Anne, Love Unearthed

A Sweet Friends to Lovers Romance

Kerri Kastle

Kerri Kastle

Copyright © [2004] by [Kerri Kastle]

All rights reserved.

No portion of this book may be reproduced in any form without written permission from the publisher or author, except as permitted by U.S. copyright law.

Contents

1. Chapter One — 1
2. Chapter Two — 13
3. Chapter Three — 24
4. Chapter Four — 33
5. Chapter Five — 41
6. Chapter Six — 51
7. Chapter Seven — 61
8. Chapter Eight — 71
9. Chapter Nine — 79
10. Chapter Ten — 89
11. Chapter Eleven — 99
12. Chapter Twelve — 113
13. Chapter Thirteen — 121
14. Chapter Fourteen — 130

15.	Chapter Fifteen	136
16.	Chapter Sixteen	143
17.	Chapter Seventeen	151
18.	Chapter Eighteen	160
19.	Chapter Nineteen	169
20.	Chapter Twenty	177
21.	Chapter Twenty-One	185
22.	Chapter Twenty-Two	193
Epilogue		201

Chapter One

Lady Anne Eversley was undeniably pleased beyond measure. Years of poring over historical articles and books in her parents' grand library had yielded a thoroughly profound result. Finally, she could transform her interests from a major hobby that imbued her daily life into a profitable occupation. She felt a rush of delight racing through her as her eyes raked over the letter in her hand a second time.

Dearest Lady Anne,

Corresponding with you on matters of history in relation to England and countries all over the world has been an illuminating experience. You may be young, but you possess a keen intelligence that extends beyond that of your peers.

In that regard, I would like to inform you that I've secured employment for you at an archaeological dig along Kensington Avenue. Although you're an esteemed lady and, no doubt, will face obstructions that might affect your ability to take up this position, I feel compelled to share the news regardless. It would be an excellent opportunity to gain practical experience and amplify your repertoire of historical knowledge.

Regrettably, the position will not remain free for long, therefore I urge you to begin as soon as you can. I am certain you'll act brilliantly and come upon useful discoveries.

Yours most sincerely,

Nigel Sheridan

Born to a common shop owner in a tiny village in the eastern part of England, Mr. Sheridan had built his wealth through imports along the Celtic and North Seas. Now rich and comfortable, he could have contented himself with living lavishly in his mansion with his beautiful wife, Lady Janet Mawley. Instead, he had joined The Society of Antiquaries of London as a wealthy researcher and sponsor, and he now managed its affairs as the President.

Her first correspondence with him had been tentative, and she had not expected much by way of response. However, Mr. Sheridan had overlooked the obvious fact of her gender and engaged her in scholarly discourse as he would with a gentleman. It was clear that he valued her opinion; although he was considerably older, she regarded him as a friend.

Now he was providing her with a rare opportunity, one she wasn't inclined to easily let go. Anne was suddenly overcome by an urgency to accept the offer before it slipped away.

"Employment at an archaeological dig," her younger cousin, Tessa, read aloud as she peered over Anne's shoulder. "This is the sort of opportunity you've always dreamed of, is it not?"

"Now and always," Anne replied with an earnest note in her voice. Her parents had passed their love of historical knowledge down to her, and she continued to nurture it even after their death.

"I don't imagine it pays handsomely," Tessa remarked. "An occupation of this kind requires high levels of interest to sustain it."

"Then it's a good thing I have plenty of that," Anne said, tucking the letter into her reticule. "I also do not mind the wage. By earning any amount at all, no matter how little, I'll have distinguished myself from most ladies of my age and class."

"That may be true, but I remain doubtful of your chances of being granted permission," Tessa said with a pitying look.

"Why is that the case?"

Tessa let out a huff of annoyance as she continued matter-of-factly, "Father has grown much stricter lately, no doubt due to his new wife hogging all his attention and insisting that his wards be married off."

Anne pursed her lips and furrowed her eyebrows contemplatively. "Uncle George may have fallen in love, but he isn't negligent."

"What if he refuses to grant you leave to work?"

"He will not," Anne answered confidently. "In fact, I'm of the mind to discuss the subject with him right away."

The trip from her bedroom to her uncle's study took only a couple of minutes. Sunlight filtered through the windows, bouncing off the chandeliers and circular mirrors. Anne hurried along the spacious hallway, excited to share her news.

She had never known her uncle to refuse her requests. He had been assigned as her ward upon the death of her parents, a duty he'd handled smoothly for the past 10 years. He was supportive and shared her parents' zeal for knowledge.

She entered the study and found her uncle, the Viscount of Rutherford, seated behind his desk. He had a patient look on his face even as his new wife, Bernice, chattered non-stop about the Geolt ball, an event they had all recently attended.

"The dance floor was especially magical," Bernice sighed appreciatively, twisting a lock of her blonde hair between her fingers. "It was smooth and gave the impression that one was gliding on ice."

"That sounds very beautiful, dear," Anne's uncle replied dutifully, pushing his spectacles further along his nose bridge. Although he didn't seem the least bit interested in his wife's long-winded statements, he was too polite to interrupt.

His decision to marry the flamboyant Bernice Tilbury had come as a shock to all. George's scholarly self seemed wrongly paired with the extravagant and garrulous Bernice. Despite Anne's reservations regarding the union, she was glad that it had resulted in making her uncle happy.

"Lady Stanhope appeared in the most dreadful gown, managing to surpass the disaster of her previous one. I cannot say it came as a surprise, given her awful fashion sense."

"Most certainly, dear."

"May I interrupt this conversation?" Anne asked, closing the door behind her.

Her aunt spoke up before her uncle could, clapping her hands in delight. "This is a lovely occurrence! I was only seconds away from asking a maid to send for you."

"Is there a matter you wish to discuss?"

"Anne, it appears you were the highlight of the Geolt ball! The previous night's newspaper proclaimed you the belle of the ball. Do you know what this means?"

"More attention, no doubt," Anne answered, feelings of dread pushing up to the surface. She had never been the sort to covet fame and popularity, preferring instead to study her books and ruminate on theories.

Bernice rolled her eyes. "It means that of all the girls present that day, you were the prettiest. More suitors shall soon begin stopping by to court you, without a doubt."

Anne bit back her objections and turned her attention to her uncle instead. "I'd like to discuss an urgent matter, my lord."

Uncle George raised an eyebrow as if to question her formal manner. "What is it, dear?"

"Mr. Sheridan wrote to me, sharing news of an open job position."

Bernice glanced at her in puzzlement. "For the servants?"

Anne shook her head. "For me. It would be a brilliant avenue to put all the knowledge I've gathered over the years into practice."

She produced the letter and handed it to her uncle, who studied the paper with an indecipherable look.

"I plan to start immediately if you would be so kind as to grant me permission."

"Paupers seek employment, not classed ladies," Bernice hissed in disapproval. "If the ton somehow gained wind of this, the Eversley household would be scandalized and disgraced!"

Anne met her aunt's gaze directly. "I am within my rights to pursue my interests, and I will not be made to feel guilty about it."

"Nigel Sheridan is an honest man, and his recommendations tend to be beneficial," Uncle George began slowly. "However, it would be considered improper for you to enter employment."

"It's a thoroughly ridiculous notion, one you ought to reject outrightly, George!" Bernice urged. "It is my wish to see your daughters and niece wedded to suitable gentlemen. Anne is 20 and will be better off married."

Anne pressed her lips together. "That decision should be mine to make."

"You might have done so already if your head wasn't filled with needless distractions." Her aunt countered.

"I have every intention of furthering my interests in history and other subjects, regardless of what you say."

"You're a beautiful girl who has already garnered a lot of male interest," Bernice cried out. "You only have to cease this nonsense to secure a more profitable future."

"My parents left a fortune behind, enough for me to live on even without a husband," Anne replied, crossing her arms. "I am neither desperate nor hasty."

Bernice shook her head. "You're terribly stubborn and ignorant of the ways of the ton. A lifetime of disgrace and dishonor awaits you if you continue down this path."

"That is a risk I'm willing to take if—"

Her uncle cleared his throat, ushering the room into silence. "You have my permission to take employment at the archaeological dig, Anne. However, there's a condition you must fulfill." He moved a pile of papers from the center of his desk to a chiffonier behind him before continuing. "Your aunt is right to be concerned about your reputation, given the rules of modern society. I do not wish to see you humiliated by the judgemental individuals who make up the ton."

"In that case, what do you suggest?" Anne asked warily.

"A steady suitor, especially one with an esteemed reputation, has the added benefit of shielding against gossip and uncharitable talk. Additionally, the idea of you navigating the streets of London without a chaperone makes me uncomfortable." Uncle George explained as he met her gaze firmly. "I'll grant you leave to take the job, but only if you acquire an honorable suitor who would be willing to accompany you to your place of employment."

"I only have a few days left before I am expected to start. I couldn't possibly find a suitor and convince him to accept those terms in such a limited timeframe."

Her uncle shrugged determinedly. "I'm afraid that's all I'm willing to say on the subject."

Bernice smiled victoriously. "It's as generous a proposition as any other."

Anne left her uncle's study with an unshakeable inkling that she'd won the battle but lost the war. She'd been allowed to work, but only if she fulfilled a condition that seemed nearly impossible.

She was not ready to marry yet, so finding a suitor was out of the question. Moreover, her family would only accept someone honorable, someone whom they could trust to keep her reputation safe. Unsure of how to make her uncle's condition happen, Anne retired to her bedroom and began writing to her sensible cousin, Felicity, for advice.

***

Cedric Steele, the Earl of Stonehaven, bore a deep-rooted dislike for extensive journeys. He wasn't in the habit of traveling long distances except in the most urgent of circumstances. Since departing his family home in Devonshire, he'd made several stops in Somerset, Axminster, and Reading.

Why had three of his cousins chosen to wed in the same month? It was both inconsiderate and impractical. His trip to London had been delayed considerably in favor of attending the weddings, and although he was now back on the road, it would be a few more days before his eventual arrival.

The post chaise drew to a halt without warning. Cedric straightened in his seat and shifted the blinds aside, recognizing the typical courtyard of a coaching inn. The scent of roasted fish and spirits lingered in the air, adding to the promise of a well-deserved rest.

"I'll check if there are available rooms, my lord," his valet announced, stepping out of the vehicle. He soon disappeared behind the heavy wooden doors of the inn.

"We are stopping for the night," Cedric said, shaking his younger brother awake. Rhys stirred at first, then he opened his eyes and nodded in acknowledgment.

"It is a long-awaited respite. How long was I asleep for?"

"Slightly over three hours," Cedric answered. "I am deeply envious of your ability to nap at any given moment."

Rhys set a top hat over his dark curls and straightened out the wrinkles in his shirt. "I learned the skill during my time at Oxford and mastered it over years of practice as a man of law."

"You've garnered quite a reputation for legal competence," Cedric commended. "It has made you a wealthy man."

"So says the individual who owns and raises one of the most sought-after breeds of horses in England," his brother replied with a proud twinkle in his eye. "I mean to replace my hackney for a thoroughbred soon."

"A racing horse?"

"They're trendy these days," Rhys said, lifting his shoulders in a shrug. "I seldom indulge in material pleasures; therefore, I shall allow myself this."

"Thoroughbreds are renowned for being spirited and agile. Is that truly a decision you want to make?"

"I may be average at horse riding, but I've been told I can convince just about anyone or anything, horses included."

Cedric stared at his brother in disbelief. "Do you truly plan on starting a discourse with the animal?"

Rhys opened the door of their carriage. "I'll pat and cajole the thoroughbred so it does my bidding, and if that fails, I'll ride it and contend with the possibility of a broken back."

"You are a madman." Cedric declared with a shake of his head. He alighted from the vehicle with more energy than he cared to spend, his boots landing on the smoothened ground with a thud.

Rhys grinned. "One needs to be if they desire to succeed as a barrister."

The two men stepped into the threshold of the coaching inn, where Cedric's valet was waiting.

"I have secured the best suites available, along with a private dining room for meals," he informed them.

"Thank you, Smith," Cedric said, patting the man on the shoulder appreciatively.

The common room was spacious and lively, as other travelers eased their weariness with loud conversation and tumblers of ale. A large fireplace sat in the center of the room, casting it in warmth and light.

With a promise to meet in the dining room after changing their clothes, the brothers retired to their respective suites. Cedric eyed his bed, debating whether to take a nap or postpone it for later. He decided it would be best to eat first and have his sleep after.

He traded his heavy tailcoat for a nightshirt just as a knock came at his door. "Who is it?"

"Smith, Your Lordship. A newly delivered letter requires your attention."

If anyone would send a letter and have it timed perfectly to his arrival, it was his father, the Duke of Devonshire. He opened the door and took the letter, his eyes narrowing at the incorrect address.

Cedric turned to his valet with a questioning look. "Are you certain this letter is for me?"

Smith tugged at his ear. "It appears so, Your Lordship. I was told to deliver it to the earl."

What were the odds of two earls lodging in the same local coaching inn at the same time? It wasn't a regular occurrence, but it also wasn't out of place. Moreover, his curiosity was already piqued, so he continued to read.

Dear Felicity,

I hope this letter finds you well and that your honeymoon was lovely. I would ordinarily await your return, but this is an urgent subject, and your advice is paramount.

My passion for history and similar subjects has yielded an incredible outcome. I have been offered a position at an archaeological dig, to supervise and analyze the discovered items. Uncle George has permitted me to take the position, on the condition that I acquire an honorable suitor willing to accompany me during the course of my employment.

As you must already suspect, I am rightly puzzled and unsure of what to do. I have no suitor in whom I am particularly interested. Even if I were to find one, I'm doubtful he'd be willing to set aside his daily tasks and interests on my behalf. This job is an opportunity of a lifetime, one I'm not inclined to so easily set aside.

Dearest cousin, could you proffer some advice? You are, after all, an endless sea of practical advice and knowledge. I look forward to your unique perspective on the matter.

Ever your loving cousin,

Anne Eversley

The owner of the letter seemed to be in a truly difficult situation, Cedric mused. In addition, it was a shame that her missive had been delivered wrongly to him.

Cedric set the paper on his bedside table and buttoned the closures of his nightshirt. He didn't know who Anne was, and by extension, her burdens weren't his to carry. He exited his suite and went to the dining room, where Rhys was already seated.

"Supper is yet to be served," Rhys said. "We'll have to wait a few minutes."

"I have missed London greatly, and I fear no one will understand the true extent of it." Cedric shared as he settled in a chair opposite his brother.

"How could I not?" Rhys teased. "I have only heard you state it nearly a million times."

"Two of my Arabians have been registered to participate in prominent horse races. I want to be in attendance when the events begin."

"Who did you sell them to?"

"Lord Ashton and Lord Kensington."

"I've heard Lord Ashton in particular, has an impressive racing stable."

Cedric nodded. "Indeed, he does. My stallions are renowned for their speed and stamina. If they do well at the races, other lords would be inclined to purchase their racehorses from me."

"Finally," Rhys sighed in relief as their meals were served. "I was only seconds away from seeking an alternate food source."

"I doubt your search would prove successful. There isn't another inn or bar in sight; therefore, you'd have to walk several miles to taste a warm meal."

Rhys cut a piece of meat and chewed carefully before replying, "With any luck, I'd go missing, which would grant me a valid reason to be absent at Mother's ball."

"What ball? Cedric asked.

Rhys groaned and ran a tired hand over his face. "Do you truly have no knowledge of it? Poor thing. Mother intends on throwing a ball in our dear sister Daphne's name, but the main and hidden goal of it is to find you a wife."

Although his mother had urged him regularly to get married, he had not expected her to take on such an elaborate scheme. It was an unsanctioned and impolite measure, one he was not in agreement with.

In addition, there was also that rumor going around about him…he thought before shaking the idea out of his head. There was no point dwelling on that when he could consider other topics.

After dinner, Cedric returned to his room for a proper night's rest. He was unable to keep the news from Rhys away from his mind. A sudden idea occurred to him, one that could potentially sabotage his meddling mother's plans.

Cedric picked up the letter he had earlier tossed aside and began writing a reply to Anne Eversley.

Chapter Two

Anne was yet to receive a reply from her cousin Felicity. She had spent the recent days hastily checking every new letter delivered to the house, to no avail. If anyone had an inkling of how to resolve difficult situations, it was Felicity.

Her cousin's intelligence lay in navigating real-world problems and exercising her cunning when occasion demanded it. In comparison, Anne was sheltered and more suited to theoretical analysis.

As she descended the stairs, she heard the sound of chairs being pulled back as her family sat for breakfast. The aroma of freshly baked bread filled the dining room, intermixing with the fragrance of cheese and fresh fruit.

"Good morning, everyone," Anne greeted, taking a seat.

"Lovely, you're awake," Bernice said, her face lighting up. "There's a lot I'd like to discuss with you."

"Today's jam is delicious," Tessa noted, slathering some of it on her bread. "Have you tried it yet, Father?"

Uncle George nodded his approval. "I have, and you're correct about its taste. The jam isn't homemade. It was a gift from a friend who traveled to America."

Alix, the second of Uncle George's three daughters, spoke up. "I would like to visit America. We're urged not to appreciate their ways, but I daresay it's intriguing in unique aspects."

Bernice's lips thinned in disapproval. "Talk of America is moot. You girls will be married to distinguished gentlemen and honor tradition, unlike our counterparts across the sea."

"The country isn't entirely lawless," Alix said, shaking her head. "I fear we English are much too judgmental and rigid in our ways."

"Enough of this," Bernice declared with a note of finality, her eyes settling on Anne. "I have commissioned a dressmaker to make you high-quality gowns in the latest fashion. Once we have decided on a date for measurements, you and I will visit her store."

It was not lost on Anne that her aunt believed the subject of her employment was a foregone issue. Not only was Bernice wrong, but her skepticism caused Anne to be even more determined to find a practical solution and begin working at the archaeological site.

"Have you read the morning newspaper yet?" She asked, turning to her uncle. "A group of industrialists have released word of a new invention. It is said to be capable of recording a person's heartbeat."

Her uncle leaned closer in interest. "That seems complicated. What is the purpose of it?"

"It aids in listening to sounds produced by the heart and lungs," Anne explained. "It will assist in diagnosing medical conditions."

"That sounds incredibly important."

"It is," she replied before adding, "Without a doubt, it's a great scientific achievement."

"I believe this invention will be widely accepted into society, unlike its recent counterpart, the dandy horse," Uncle George said with a hint of amusement.

"The heart recorder is undeniably practical."

Uncle George nodded in agreement. "Meanwhile, the dandy horse is dangerous to maneuver and only used by wealthy aristocrats with change to spare."

Anne enjoyed the regular exchange of information with her uncle. She was grateful that upon her parents' death, her guardianship had gone to her father's brother and not someone who would have stifled her intelligence.

"You girls have been invited to a ball hosted by another of my friends, Lady Liselle," Bernice announced, filling the silence. "Perhaps one of you will catch the eye of an eligible gentleman."

Anne bit back a groan. "May I be excused from the ball? I have plans for that day."

"I haven't even mentioned the date yet!" Bernice exclaimed, looking insulted.

"Regardless, I feel compelled to inform you in advance of my absence."

"Your insolence is totally unacceptable!" Bernice spluttered. "George, say something!"

Uncle George released a sigh. "I love you very much, Anne. Bernice does too, which is why she wishes to see you married and well-settled." He glanced off to the side with a pensive look. "Sometimes I wonder if I have filled your head with too many books, which is why you're so reluctant to participate in events other ladies jump at."

"I was always going to turn out this way, regardless of your involvement, dear Uncle," replied Anne without missing a beat. She had been born to a family of readers who enjoyed intellectual pursuits, after all.

Before their accident, her parents were historians who traveled the world for their research. They had bequeathed their entire library to her, their only child, along with a vast estate she would gain access to upon turning 21.

"Moreover, I don't believe I have acted scandalously," Anne continued. "I desire only to be permitted to explore my interests. I am also not opposed to marriage. I simply haven't found a suitable gentleman."

"What, pray tell, do you look for in a gentleman?" Her uncle questioned.

Anne retrieved her pocketbook from her draw bag and jotted down a few attributes. She nodded in a satisfied way, then picked her book up and began reading what she'd written.

"I want a gentleman who loves me for who I am. By that, I don't mean someone who merely tolerates my hobbies and makes attempts to change me," she explained, frowning at the unpleasant thought. "He must be honorable, considerate, and trustworthy."

"That's a reasonable list," Uncle George admitted. "With any luck, such a gentleman will swoop in soon to sweep you off your feet."

"Perhaps I'll find him while working at the archaeological dig," Anne tried.

"The condition I've set remains," her uncle said firmly. "You are not to begin until you've found a legitimate suitor who will accompany you."

After breakfast, Anne lingered in the hallway. She couldn't keep from wondering how to acquire a suitor within the limited timeframe. She had no desire to lead an innocent gentleman to believe she was interested in him, but there seemed to be no other option.

The butler approached her with an item in hand. "There's a letter for you, my lady."

"Thank you, Barnaby," she replied, unable to keep the excitement from her voice. She waited till she had reached her bedroom before opening the letter.

Anne was puzzled and disappointed to learn that it wasn't from Felicity. Instead, the letter had been signed by a gentleman whose name she'd heard mentioned a few times.

My Lady,

I considered it a surprising development when my valet handed over your letter. It didn't take long for me to realize it had been misdelivered to me. It is undeniably a grave error on the part of the postal messengers, but I assure you the details you shared are safe with me.

I'm writing to see if you would be willing to consider an unusual proposition. Your desire to gain employment in an area of interest is only natural and worthy of pursuit. The conditions you've been provided with may be difficult—but they can be fulfilled with proper strategy.

I want to propose a fake courtship, which will allow each of us to indulge in our interests without the unwanted meddling of guardians or parents. I know this is sudden and perhaps shocking at first glance, but I urge you to consider the idea.

I humbly request your presence at the giant cherry tree in Linton Park next morning so that we can discuss the idea further.

With sincerest regards,

Cedric Steele, Earl of Stonehaven

Anne held the letter in disbelief. The Earl of Stonehaven was a powerful man. He was the first-born son of the Duke of Devonshire and in line to inherit the title.

He had wrongly received Felicity's letter and instead of ignoring it, he'd chosen to write her back. What would motivate a man such as him to propose a fake courtship? Anne wondered.

Regardless of his intentions, she was desperate enough to consider his offer. Anne made up her mind to visit Linton Park the following morning.

***

The morning sun spied through curtained windows as Cedric reclined in the drawing room and busied himself with a book. A persistent snipping sound filled the room as his younger sister, Daphne, trimmed the edges of the material she was embroidering.

Cedric enjoyed peaceful moments such as this when he could relax and be surrounded by family. The book in his hands provided an in-depth explanation of the best horse breeding techniques, a subject which interested him immensely.

He was determined to put his new knowledge to use when raising his next batch of stallions. With any luck, that would result in champion racehorses that many gentlemen would vie against one another to purchase.

His mother walked into the room with a delighted smile on her face.

"It is not often that we get to gather in one spot like this," she said. "It's a shame your father prefers the countryside over London. Otherwise, we'd be completely reunited. Where's Rhys?"

"He left for a meeting with a legal associate," Daphne replied without glancing up from her embroidering.

His mother stood behind his armchair and peered at the cover of his book. "I don't suppose you've traded your hobby for a better one, although I had hoped that would be the case."

Cedric flipped a page. "I do not recall giving you the impression that I'd act differently."

"Horse races are entirely too dangerous and coarse for a proper gentleman," she chided. "My wish is that you'll take a wife instead and overcome that vice."

"The world has changed since you were a sickly child with a fear of horses, Mother," Cedric replied collectedly. "My interest in horse races is not only because of the events themselves but also due to my involvement in breeding prizewinning horses. You would know this if you didn't shun the topic entirely."

"In today's society, the ownership of a stud farm that produces quality horses leads to prestige and wealth. Cedric has earned both." Daphne pointed out.

"It's still a futile endeavor," his mother insisted, not one to overcome her prejudices easily. "But I shall cease haranguing you over it for now."

"Your carriage is ready, my lord," a footman announced, entering the room.

Cedric set his book on a Pembroke table and arose from his seat. "Perfect. I'm heading out, Mother."

"I didn't know you were leaving the townhouse ..." his mother trailed off before a look of determination replaced her expression of bewilderment. "Where are you going?"

Cedric raised an eyebrow at the unusual behavior. "I need to run a quick errand, after which I'll visit the stud farm. Why?"

"I invited Lady Janet to spend some time at the house this afternoon. Do you remember her? She's a quiet and pleasant girl from a renowned family."

Cedric's face twitched in barely concealed annoyance at another of his mother's schemes. By inviting a lady of her choosing to the house, she hoped he would fall in love and provide her with the grandchildren she so clearly desired.

"I'm sure she is," he replied blandly. "That will be all, and I shall now take my leave."

"You can't. Lady Janet expressed a fervent desire to meet you, and I promised to fulfill that need."

"Perhaps another time," Cedric said. "I'm leaving the house to see a lady who I'm certain will be of greater interest than Lady Janet."

That caught his mother's attention. Her jaw fell open, and it took a few good seconds to gather herself. "You must tell me who it is at once." She demanded.

"I must confess, dear brother, I am curious to know who it is as well," Daphne said. She halted her embroidering and tilted her head at him curiously.

"I'll only reveal the information when the time is right."

His mother drew closer. "I swear to you, I shall keep it a secret."

"The more you insist on knowing, the more I am tempted to cease speaking to the lady," Cedric replied pointedly. "Do not force my hand, Mother."

Lady Lavinia recognized the subtle threat at once. She sighed loudly and waved her hand in surrender. "Whatever you say, son. I wish you the best in all endeavors, this one especially."

Cedric emerged from his townhouse with a triumphant grin on his face. So far, all was going according to plan. His mother may have ceased questioning him, but she would undoubtedly do everything in her power to discover the information herself. It was just as he intended.

Lady Anne Eversley was the final piece of his plan. Once news spread that he was courting her, everyone would stop pressuring him to marry. As his carriage hurtled along the smooth path leading into Linton Park, he hoped Lady Eversley had accepted his request to meet.

He waited under the giant cherry tree, a plant rumored to have been planted centuries ago. He resisted the urge to pace back and forth and berated himself for neglecting to bring the book he'd been reading prior along.

How long would it take for Lady Eversley to arrive? he wondered idly. Minutes? Hours?

The familiar sound of an approaching coach provided the answer. The vehicle rolled to a stop next to his, accompanied by the neighing of horses.

A lady emerged from its interior, carefully assisted by her footman. She scanned the area, and when her eyes landed on him, she ventured forward in his direction. That was the confirmation he needed that she was Lady Eversley. She was accompanied by what appeared to be her lady's maid, a solemn-looking girl in an unremarkable gown.

Lady Eversley, on the other hand, made the yellow gown she was wearing seem like a glorious work of art. She was classically beautiful, with wavy blonde hair and round blue eyes that peered eagerly from a sculptured oval face.

"It's a pleasure to meet you, Lord Stonehaven," she ventured before he could introduce himself.

She was bold and confident, Cedric noted. He fixed her a polite smile and bowed his head slightly. "The pleasure is entirely mine, Lady Eversley. Feel free to address me by my first name, Cedric. With any luck, we'll be seeing more of each other henceforth."

"You may call me Anne," she replied before gesturing to the girl beside her. "This is my lady's maid, Polly. I trust her wholly, and I assure you she'll say no word of this meeting to anyone."

"I'm honored to be in your presence, my lord," Polly said.

It was clear that Polly knew the reason he and Anne had chosen to meet and was in agreement with her mistress's rebellious gesture.

Cedric nodded at her in acknowledgment before turning his attention back to Anne. "Am I to assume you agree with the idea I proposed in the letter?"

"I'm desperate, and time is running out," Anne admitted. "I have little choice but to consider your proposal. However, I must ask why you've chosen to partake in a fake courtship."

"In true stereotypical fashion, my mother is relentless about seeing her older son wedded and happily settled," Cedric explained with a casual lift of his shoulder. "We are both headstrong individuals, you see. I am equally determined to fight off the wave of prospective ladies being pushed my way. A fake courtship will cause my mother to believe I'm interested in someone and halt her scheming."

He had a few good years left before he was ready to settle down and start a family, which he planned to enjoy to the fullest. Moreover, none of his friends were married yet and he wasn't interested in being the first to begin down that path.

"That is completely understandable," Anne responded. "You already know why I'm inclined to pursue this option. Scientific exploits are a rarity in this day and age, mainly because half of the population has been shut out from it. My interest in history and archaeology is one I hope to nurture during the course of my employment."

"Our society is late in realizing the value of women, especially in non-traditional fields, and I hope that changes soon," Cedric said, tipping his head in sympathy. "I, too, have a field of interest: horse breeding. I raise thoroughbreds to participate in races."

"That sounds unique," Anne replied politely, but he caught the lack of interest in her voice. "There's a lot to be said about the craftsmanship of discovered artifacts and how they provide a nuanced view of how our predecessors lived."

After a thorough observation of Anne, Cedric decided she'd serve as a good partner for a fake engagement. She might be strikingly beautiful, but she wasn't in love with him, and it was unlikely that she would ever be.

They were two contradicting individuals who hardly shared similar interests. Cedric had found himself growing bored when she began speaking about artifacts and made historical references. Similarly, she didn't give a fig about horseracing and its surrounding details. It was the perfect arrangement.

He accepted Anne's offer of a handshake with a smile. "Now that it's been established that we're both in agreement with a fake courtship, what do you suggest as our first course of action?"

"I'd like to introduce you to my family, specifically my uncle," Anne said. "I invite you to visit my home the following evening and join us for a game of battledore and shuttlecocks."

"I'll be there," Cedric promised.

Chapter Three

Anne glanced thoughtfully at the assortment of gowns on her bed, where she'd laid them side by side for easier comparison. Each ensemble was distinct in size, shaping, and color. She picked up a blue gown and nodded in approval before setting it aside.

Choosing outfits for work at the archaeological site was necessary. She had decided to avoid flashy, expensive gowns and wear comfortable, practical ones instead. She was aware that the wealthier a person seemed, the less friendly they would be perceived as by others.

Anne had received a bronze brooch to use as a means of identification when visiting the dig. It had accompanied Mr. Nigel's letter and now sat in her drawer, ready for use.

She felt excited and relieved to be in her current position. She couldn't keep from musing about her great privilege. Highly-born young ladies were discouraged from acquiring any sort of employment. They were left with no choice but to content themselves with seeking beneficial marital unions and preparing for wifehood.

Her uncle might be grumpy and unyielding, but he'd granted her a chance other guardians wouldn't even consider. She was grateful to him for that.

When compared with other occupations in London, hers was barely tasking. She had to work only three days a week and report regularly to The Society of Antiquaries of London.

The previous day's meeting with Cedric, Lord Stonehaven, had gone smoothly. The earl was adamant about not getting married, which was why he'd suggested a fake courtship. A distinctly handsome man with broad shoulders that spoke to an active lifestyle, thick raven-black hair, and stormy gray eyes, he had a surprisingly affable personality.

Anne had a good feeling about Cedric, which was relieving. Given his title and esteemed reputation, it was likely that her family would be accepting of him.

A knock on the door brought her out of her thoughts.

"Is that you, Polly? Do come in."

Her lady's maid entered the room, carrying an array of newly purchased gowns. "Your aunt asked me to bring these to you. She wants you to pick a gown from this collection and wear it for the evening."

"I already have a gown to wear."

Polly nodded. "Clothes are never a waste. I'll place them in your wardrobe for future use."

Anne drew closer and hugged her. "You're the best lady's maid anyone could ever wish for, Polly."

"I'm much too devoted to you and your unconventional ways," Polly pointed out with an amused look. "I will not be receiving any awards for the best lady's maid if there ever was such a thing."

"You aren't a grumpy crone, and you're more sensible than most people," Anne replied, tugging a dark blue riding skirt over her slender hips.

"Where are you going?"

"I intend to take my horse for a spirited trot in Regent's Park."

"Good luck with that," Polly said, glancing up from the pile of clothes she'd begun folding. "I doubt your aunt will let you make it as far as the door."

"She'll have to catch me first," Anne responded before exiting the room. She was properly dressed in a woolen riding habit intermixed with gray and blue. She'd spent a lot of time in the library lately, and some time outdoors was precisely what she needed to balance her internal activity wheel.

Her riding boots made a soft thumping sound as she walked down the hall. It must have alerted her aunt, who hurried into view and eyed her clothing with a look of alarm. "You can't just leave the house, Anne!"

"I'll be back within the hour," she replied, adjusting the ends of her gloves. "A quick horse ride through the park, and that's it."

"You ought to be preparing for your suitor's arrival! Lord Stonehaven will be here any minute."

"I already have a gown picked out, and I doubt Lord Stonehaven will mind a bit of lateness," Anne said reasonably.

It was clear Bernice meant to debate the matter further, but her need to set the house in order before Cedric's arrival was more paramount. "I don't have time to argue. The napkins are yet to be arranged properly. Make sure you return before your suitor gets here," she finished, wagging a finger in Anne's direction.

"I'll do my best," Anne replied simply before departing the house.

***

Cedric's coach halted in front of the grand townhouse belonging to the Eversleys. Only a few prominent families still owned such spacious townhouses, constructed before London became so densely populated. His family's townhouse was similar, although Cedric preferred the polished granite of the Eversley walls.

He wasted no time in walking up to the main door. He had arrived on time, distinctly well-dressed with properly coiffed hair, polished buttons, and a neatly tied cravat.

The fact that it was a fake courtship didn't mean he couldn't put his best foot forward, Cedric mused. If anything, doing so would add to the impression that the relationship between him and Anne was real.

He knocked on the door and raised an impressed eyebrow when it swung open a second later. A tall man with a full head of graying hair stood in the doorway. He bowed his head in respect before announcing in a clear, baritone voice, "My Lord, The Earl of Stonehaven!"

Cedric nodded in acknowledgment. A footman stepped forward to take his coat just as a robust older lady with auburn hair and extravagant jewelry appeared.

"Lord Stonehaven, as the lady of this household, I welcome you to our peaceful abode," she greeted.

"Thank you, Lady Rutherford. Your home is tastefully decorated and a pleasure to be in."

"The viscount and I are glad to have you join us for a game of battledore and shuttlecocks," she continued, leading him down the hall until they reached an exit leading to the back of the house. "I would much rather attend a soirée than play around in the sun, but Lord Rutherford and his girls consider it an enjoyable pastime."

There was a judgmental edge in her voice, one he was smart enough to ignore. Instead, he replied politely, "I'm honored to be included in this activity for the evening."

"Good. Let us join the others."

The patio was airy and enclosed by brick walls, with a blooming garden to the right and a paved area to the left. Two ladies stood off to the side, both giggling as they hit a feather shuttlecock toward each other. A tall man with graying long hair sat on a bench, his head turning in their direction as they approached. Cedric recognized the Viscount of Rutherford at once, having glimpsed him several times at events.

"Look, dear, the Earl's here," Lady Rutherford said to her husband.

"I'm delighted to meet the man who has finally caught Anne's eye," Lord Rutherford said, shaking his head firmly. "It must have been no easy feat. You're welcome to our home, Lord Stonehaven."

"Thank you for the invitation, sir," Cedric replied with a winning smile, "Perhaps one day we'll discuss the true story of Anne and myself over drinks."

"State the date, and I'll be there," Lord Rutherford responded, giving him a hearty slap on the back. "Over there are my daughters, Tessa and Alix," he continued, beckoning the ladies over. "The oldest, Felicity, is due to return from her honeymoon soon."

Lady Tessa and Lady Alix had the signature blonde hair of the Eversley family, although Lady Alix's was of a darker shade. They greeted him with a mix of politeness and barely concealed excitement, their eyes darting to each other in unspoken communication.

Lady Rutherford cleared her throat in a gesture that demanded attention. "Our Anne is a delightful girl who prefers to spend time gardening and perfecting her embroidery."

Cedric raised a skeptical brow. "Truly?"

Lady Rutherford nodded. "She enjoys being around children and will make a good wife. You must be wondering about her whereabouts. She went for a peaceful and slow horse ride in Regent's Park."

Cedric could tell that Anne's aunt was attempting to depict her niece as a traditional woman with conventional interests. Unfortunately, it was a futile attempt, given that he already had an inkling of her personality.

Just then, Anne entered through the back gates. She was dressed in a riding habit, her hair tossed in a messy bun. She took notice of him and drew closer.

"I apologize for keeping you waiting," she murmured breathlessly, yet to recover from her outdoor exertion.

"That's quite alright, my lady. I believe I've managed to avail myself in your absence by meeting your family."

"We're a competitive sort, but we'll lessen that for the sake of your enjoyment."

"Don't do so on my account," he encouraged. "You'll find that I'm equally competitive when it comes to sporting activities."

"Anne! It's impolite to be dressed inappropriately with a visitor present," Lady Rutherford chided in a half-whisper, which was easily overheard by everyone present.

"I'll be back," Anne mouthed to him as her aunt tugged her indoors for a change of clothes.

Cedric chuckled to himself and joined Lord Rutherford for a game. The viscount was skilled at hitting the shuttlecock, but his aim was less accurate. He was also less forceful, unlike Cedric, who had perfected his hits through years of playing with Rhys. The game ended at a tally of 150 to 138, with Cedric snagging the win.

"You're a good player," Lord Rutherford praised as the two men sat down for a break.

"You have a good swinging arm," Tessa added, nodding her approval.

"I would like to challenge your lordship to a game," Alix ventured, a competitive glint in her eye.

"Careful, she's the best player of us all," Anne warned as she joined them. She had substituted her riding habit for a comfortable blue gown that matched her eyes.

"I shall endeavor not to underestimate her," Cedric promised, picking up his battledore.

The game ended in a tie, with Alix promising to win next time. A footman brought a tray of drinks and biscuits, providing needed refreshment after a fun but tiring activity. Cedric hadn't expected to enjoy spending time with Anne's family. However, he was glad he did because it made their arrangement more tolerable.

As they reclined in their seats and sipped their drinks, Lord Rutherford turned to him with a reluctant appraisal. "It occurred to me halfway through our game that you're the same earl who is said to have an extraordinarily competitive streak, especially in horse racing," he shared slowly. "I'm glad you tamed that down for Anne's sake."

Cedric set his cup down with a pronounced thud. "My only wish is to make good memories from this new experience."

"It would be foolish to trust you when competing with your horse in a race," Lord Rutherford continued. "Outside of that, I believe you're an honorable gentleman who will act properly with Anne."

"It's still frowned upon for a couple courting to spend long hours alone together," Cedric pointed out. "The ton might not see things as charitably as you do."

"I'm aware of that," Lord Rutherford replied steadily. "However, this is the only way I can heed Anne's wishes and keep her safe.

Let them gossip or whisper. I believe both our families are reputable enough to shield against any negative consequences."

It was clear that although he put much stock in the rules and regulations that governed society, his love for his niece shone brighter.

Afterward, Anne and Cedric sat together while her family conversed in the background.

"Thank you for coming. I hope you had a great time, and I apologize for my uncle's remarks."

Cedric turned to look at her. "What remarks?"

"The ones he made regarding your competitiveness," she replied. "I noticed the way you stiffened and momentarily looked upset. Was I correct?"

"You were," Cedric admitted. "But your uncle made an innocent remark based on a rumor, and I do not hold any grudges against him for it."

"I'm assuming he was referring to a controversial event in the field of horse racing."

"He was," he replied without elaborating further. He reminded himself that this was a fake courtship and that there was no need to explain himself.

Anne tilted her head thoughtfully before saying, "You have an aura I trust, regardless of any controversy."

Cedric chuckled. "Isn't it illogical to trust someone for no good reason other than their aura?"

"Our brains are wired to make quick judgments, which are influenced by biases. Your manner of speech, your appearance, and other factors have culminated into my present perception of you," Anne responded in a logical manner. "Therefore, my behavior is perfectly reasonable."

Cedric grinned, amused. She had gone out of her way to proffer reassurance to him, even when she didn't need to, and had achieved that in a hilariously direct way.

He rose from his seat. "I must depart now. Thank you for an entertaining evening."

"My resumption is in two days," Anne reminded him. "That's on Monday."

"I shall mark the day on my calendar, my lady," he replied.

Cedric bade the Eversleys goodbye before leaving for his home. The fake courtship was turning out to be a worthwhile investment of his time.

Chapter Four

Dressed in a humble gray gown with a high neckline, Anne waited in the hallway without bothering to sit. She was ready to begin working at the dig and was nearly jumping out of her skin with excitement.

Her heart did an extra jump when she overheard Cedric's voice as he returned the butler's greetings. She had been worried about him arriving late, but he'd done nothing of the sort, and for that, she was grateful.

"Good morning, Anne," Cedric said as she walked toward him. He was neatly dressed in a gray waistcoat and black trousers, a few strands of his hair fittingly falling across his face. "Are you prepared for the day?"

"More than I have ever been."

"Excellent," her uncle praised, joining them in the hall. "With that attitude, you'll most certainly overcome obstacles heading your way."

"Good to see you again, Lord Rutherford," Cedric responded. "I promise I'll keep your niece safe."

Her uncle turned to him with a look of appreciation. "The prospect of my niece venturing along the streets of London on her own is a scary one. I'm glad you'll be by her side."

"We have to depart now or risk running late," Anne said. She bade her uncle goodbye with a kiss on the cheek before hurrying out the main door and into the carriage.

It was her first time alone in an enclosed space with a gentleman who wasn't a member of her family. It felt unusual, but not in an uncomfortable way.

"You seem happier than usual, and it doesn't take much thinking to guess why," Cedric said, breaking the silence.

Anne smiled. "I have dreamed of a day like this on several occasions, where I can contribute value and be rewarded for my labor. It's what my parents would have wanted."

"Did they share your interests?"

She nodded. "They were the pioneers, and I learned from them. My parents were historians who raised me to value scientific knowledge and research."

"That sounds like a unique upbringing."

"It was unlike any other," Anne replied softly, eyes watering as she recalled the memory. "We lived in a grand country house, read books together in the library, and took evening strolls in the garden."

Cedric gazed at her in silent concern. "Perhaps we should change the topic. My intention was not to cause you sadness."

Anne shook her head. "It's alright. It's high time we discussed our respective lives anyway. My parents died in a tragic accident at sea. I overcame the maddening grief by reading the books and articles they left behind."

"My condolences on your loss. They sound like two incredible individuals."

Anne fumbled with the collar of her gown, embarrassed to have changed the formerly amicable mood to a solemn one. She clapped her hands energetically, which earned a raised eyebrow from the handsome gentleman beside her.

Although he interacted with her as needed, she sensed a firm sense of detachment from him. Anne frowned at that. The fact that their present situation was fake didn't mean they couldn't be friends, did it?

"What are you thinking about?" Cedric questioned, and Anne realized she had been quiet for too long.

"Would you like to hear the story of how I got my job?" She blurted out, feeling an internal compulsion to keep talking.

"Certainly."

There it was again. That dutiful response from him was a habit of first-born sons raised to inherit a title and act responsibly. She'd much prefer it if he shared his true feelings instead of acting a part.

"I couldn't just read books forever. I knew I had to interact with similar-minded individuals," she explained. "I was lucky to develop a regular correspondence with an influential member of The Society of Antiquaries of London. He's helped get my articles published in multiple publications and was the one who acquired my job."

"That's rather kind of him. Not many people would go so far to help others, a lady especially."

"Is that what you truly think?"

Cedric shot her a puzzled look. "What do you mean?"

Anne pursed her lips. "I can sense that you're only responding to be polite."

"Is that a terrible thing?"

"It is. I wish to learn of your true opinion. There's no use hiding anything from me."

"How ironic," Cedric replied dryly. "Given that the premise of this relationship is based on falseness."

"That doesn't mean you should endure my statements if you have no interest in them," Anne protested. "This arrangement will be better off when one side isn't being disingenuous about his thoughts."

He released a sigh. "Well, if you insist on knowing, I find all the talk about history boring, but I recognize its importance to you."

"I appreciate you sharing your genuine thoughts," Anne replied with a shrug. "My interests are niche ones, and I do not expect everyone to care for them."

"Feel free to keep discussing your interests," Cedric encouraged. "I'm a good listener, even when the subject isn't one I'm passionate about."

"Thank you. Now that you're being expressive regarding your thoughts, I would like to know the details behind the rumor you mentioned earlier."

"It isn't something I would like to talk about," he replied, visibly hesitating.

"Are you trying to protect someone? Perhaps a love interest?"

"If only that were the case," he said dryly. "It would make my reluctance to speak more rewarding."

Their vehicle soon arrived at their destination. Anne gasped in delight as she glimpsed piles of rock and sand behind a heavy metal gate. She showed her brooch and was allowed in, with Cedric firmly by her side. She was grateful for his presence as the curious eyes of a dozen men landed on her.

They were gathered around a large trench, the depth of which she could not yet ascertain. Their faces glistened with sweat and dirt as they dug deeper with spades and picks. One of the men detached himself from the group and approached her. He was short, middle-aged, and walked with a pronounced gait.

"You must be Anne," he said with a welcoming nod. "The lady in charge of examining artifacts we discover."

"That's correct. I'm glad to be here, and so is my companion, Cedric," she replied. "What is your name?"

"It's a pleasure to meet you both. I'm called Hatter by friends and foe alike. Permit me to show you to your office, Madam."

"In a second," Anne said. She ventured forward and addressed the group of men. "Good morning, everyone! The gentleman next to me is Cedric. My name is Anne, and I'll be working with you all for the next couple of weeks."

"God bless you, my lady!" One of the men cried out, and the others laughed. They were a friendly bunch, it seemed, which caused Anne to release a sigh of relief.

Hatter led them to an enclosed space away from the noisy digging before taking his leave. It had a low ceiling and only a window to see out of, but it was tidy and functional. A sturdy desk paired with a chair stood in the middle of the room while partly empty bookshelves lined the walls. A lone chair was placed in a corner, likely for a visitor or, as in Anne's case, a companion.

"I doubt those men believe we are ordinary people choosing to play with trinkets instead of pursuing more profitable occupations," Cedric pointed out.

"They don't have to believe we're ordinary people," Anne replied. "It is better for us to pass as wealthy individuals pursuing unique interests than as titled members of society, which would make our presence scandalous."

"You may be correct."

"I *am* correct," Anne retorted, brushing past him. "In addition, I'm not here to play with trinkets. And I'd appreciate it if you refrained from touching the artifacts."

She was aware that she was being stand-offish, but surely it was to be expected after he'd compared the most impactful opportunity of her life to child's play.

Cedric walked to the lone chair and sat down before producing a book and flipping through its pages. "As a passionate person myself, I understand the need for admonition. Therefore, I shall keep from making such unfavorable comparisons."

He hadn't taken offense to her tone and had treated her outburst like a reasonable concern. Anne glimpsed the cover of his book and discerned that it was about horses. He was not wrong about being passionate, although the subjects of their interests could not be more different.

"I ought to try this training style on my horses later," he murmured more to himself than her as his eyes remained fixed on the book pages.

Anne couldn't exactly blame him for that. She had earlier wondered how he would keep himself occupied while she worked and was glad he'd found an effective task to indulge in.

The sound of approaching footsteps could be heard before Hatter appeared in the doorway. He was carrying a box, which he set on the desk with Anne's permission.

"There's a slight issue, one which could potentially affect your ability to work here," Hatter shared with a serious look.

"What is it?"

"Most of the items we've discovered seem to be unoriginal," he explained. "They break easily, and not because they've been buried in the ground for several centuries. Some look recently buried, and others are simply unremarkable to look at."

"Are you saying someone planted them for us to discover?"

Hatter shrugged. "That doesn't have to be the case. Perhaps the land once belonged to someone who liked history and purchased fake versions of items he read about."

"Do the other men agree?"

"We all do," Hatter replied. "The general assumption is that the items we've found were lost over the years and somehow ended up in the ground."

"Thank you for informing me," Anne said, emptying out the box. "The items may be unoriginal but that doesn't mean they can't be examined for further information."

Hatter departed, and the room was once again quiet except for the occasional rustle from Cedric turning the pages of his book. Anne nodded in satisfaction at the array of items on the table.

What Hatter said was merely a theory. It was up to her to confirm if it was indeed true. There were a couple of recognizable items, such as a Roman ring, figurines, spearheads, and a wide metal comb that was of dubious use. At first glance, none of the objects looked to be fake.

Only by meticulously analyzing them would she be able to tell if the men's hunch was correct. Anne retrieved her work items from the bookshelf and arranged them on the desk before standing back with a look of satisfaction. For a moderately sized site, there was an impressive number of tools to aid her research.

She picked up a magnifying glass, pleased by how nicely its handle fit in her hand. There were also rulers and measuring tapes for determining the size and shapes of the items. Lastly, there were carnets in case she needed to draw or make sketches.

It was all so new and impressive, yet she wasn't intimidated or scared. She would conduct her research unfailingly and consult her books when there were questions that needed answering. If all failed, then she'd write to Mr. Nigel seeking his assistance. After all, an individual who sought the opinion of others when necessary was more inclined to find success.

As Anne resumed examination of the historical objects, a hoarse, fear-stricken yell broke through the quiet.

"What was that?" She questioned, turning in Cedric's direction. But he was already on his feet and out of the room. Anne scurried after him, a difficult task given that his long legs seemed to cover as much ground in one step as she could in two.

They arrived at the scene of the commotion, joining the cluster of men gathered around a deep trench.

"Help!" Came that yell again. Anne drew closer, covering her mouth in a bid to hold back a startled gasp. A man angled his body along the trench wall, his foot bent unnaturally to his left. A wooden brace lay some yards away, likely having given way under his weight.

With a broken foot and no brace to balance on, the man began to slip further into the deep, rocky trench.

Chapter Five

Anne stared at the trapped man in sheer terror. The last thing she had expected to see on her first day of work was a man slowly sliding down to his death. If he was lucky, he would have to contend with a couple of cuts and broken bones. Worse, he was in danger of hitting his head against the rocks and dying a painful death.

Anne preferred the former, as did every other individual gathered, their faces heavy with alarm and pity as they watched the incident unfold.

"We have to help him," she began to say, her mind racing for workable options. The man had managed to halt his downward movement by tightly gripping a rock, but it was only a matter of time before that gave out, too. She felt a warm hand on her shoulder, tugging her back.

"Don't stand so close to the hole. Otherwise, I'll have you to worry about next," Cedric told her, a surprising dose of concern present in his eyes.

Anne did as she was bid, taking a few steps back so she was no longer teetering at the edge.

"I'm on the leaner side when compared to most of the men here, which makes me liable to enter the trench without weakening the wooden braces further," Cedric said, hastily relieving himself of his coat and waistcoat. He rolled the sleeves of his linen shirt up to his elbows and tossed his white cravat to the muddy ground.

To Anne's surprise and amazement, he set a steady foot atop a wooden brace before repeating the same action with the next one. He descended into the trench with a fluidity that reminded her of a wild cat, each step sure and controlled.

She was dimly aware of hushed murmurs and words of encouragement as everyone gathered to watch. Her eyes remained fixated on Cedric, whose descent was marked by a determined look on his face. There was no fear or anxiety—only a desire to rescue an injured individual and get him to safety. He seemed to take no notice of his ripped shirt after snagging it on a jagged piece of stone or of the harsh sun beating down on his back.

"Someone, get a rope," Anne said, relieved when one of the men paid heed to her words. She watched as Cedric stopped beside the injured man and exchanged words with him. Most likely, he was enquiring about the state of his wound and proffering needed reassurance.

The injured man nodded and let himself be helped up by Cedric. Anne held her breath as the rope was lowered, catching Cedric's notice. His hands worked skillfully, crafting the rope into a loop and slipping it under the injured man's armpits. Once he had ensured that the man was secure and comfortable, he gestured for the others to pull.

After several minutes of straining and hauling, the injured man's head appeared above the trench, accompanied by loud, victorious whoops from his colleagues.

He was dirtied and in pain from a broken foot, but otherwise, he looked fine. The only thing he required was a doctor's attention, which one of the men had rushed away to summon.

Cedric had climbed out shortly after the man, his face sweaty from exertion. The workers cast admiring glances and slapped his shoulders in appreciation. With dirty clothes and cuts along his body, he looked the very opposite of when he'd arrived that morning. Nevertheless, he was a hero who had saved someone from a possible death, and that mattered most of all.

"You did an excellent deed," Anne praised, too amazed to say anything else as he approached.

Cedric shrugged casually. "It was either that or watch the poor man slide to his death. And I could not abide that."

"Many men would bide their time and seek other alternatives before climbing into that dangerous trench," she pointed out.

"Perhaps I would, too, if I wasn't certain doing so would not harm me in any way," He admitted, patting his shirt to expel some of the dust.

"I don't believe that. I suspect you're the type to attempt saving a man from a tornado, even when there's little chance of success."

He raised an eyebrow. "So, a fool?"

"No, a hero."

That elicited a chuckle from him. "Have you been reading romantic stories in addition to your historical books?"

"Occasionally," Anne responded. "That's better than Felicity, who spends much of her time reading about handsome pirates and the like."

"Your cousin? Given that she's on her honeymoon, I'd say her interests have served her well."

"That they have. I cannot say the same for your excessive humility, but I am grateful for your presence today."

He shook his head in disagreement. "I'd argue that you've mistaken my nonchalance for humility. I do not like to expend energy on certain topics when I can simply move past them."

"Will you inform your family of what you did today?"

Cedric lifted a shoulder in a shrug. "Maybe. Maybe not. I might if someone refers to it."

"My, you really are nonchalant."

He bent briefly in a mock bow. "Only about most things. Few subjects or people ignite my genuine interest. Despite that, I've been able to hold my own in society thanks to the veneer of politeness."

That explained why he had dutifully listened to her earlier, even though he didn't truly care about what she had to say. Anne ignored the pang of hurt, concluding that it was less a statement about her and more about him.

He was a man with a fixed passion for horses and races, with little interest in other subjects. Given his privileged background, he had not been raised to pay attention to hobbies other than his own.

It was only fair, seeing as she cared little for horses and races. Still, for the sake of decent interactions between them, she was willing to learn or pay attention to his pastimes. Would he be willing to do the same?

She was too invested in this, she reprimanded herself. After all, this was a fake courtship and there was no need for extra effort on both sides.

Anne asked a pressing question that had lingered far too long on her mind. "Where did you learn to climb?"

Cedric winked. "That is one of the many skills I have under my belt."

It was clear he wasn't so willing to part with his secrets. For a man who had a relatively affable personality, he could be quite tight-lipped when he wanted to be. Unfortunately for him, Anne was the curious type who enjoyed deciphering private affairs and puzzles.

Inwardly vowing to broach the subject at a later time, Anne motioned for him to come with her to the office. She was relieved to have him by her side again and glad her first day of work hadn't resulted in a disaster after all.

"I brought a salve along with me although I hadn't expected to utilize it so quickly," She explained, digging through her reticule for the aforementioned item.

Cedric leaned back against his chair, wincing slightly with every movement. His shirt was torn in several areas, and multiple cuts lined his bruised skin.

She retrieved the salve and covered the short distance to stand in front of him. "I'd like to rub this against your scrapes if you don't mind."

"You don't have to," he replied. "I could have it tended to by a doctor when I return home."

She took his arm and dabbed the salve carefully on a cut. "Waiting around only increases the chance of an infection."

"My mother would raze the entirety of London, were that to happen."

"I wouldn't blame her. Be careful henceforth, will you?"

"This is only my third trench of the week," Cedric joked.

Anne's lips twitched in amusement. "That's thrice too many."

"This one's certainly unusable now," he said, referring to his tattered shirt. "As are the coat and waistcoat, which have been soiled by mud."

"Now that I've treated your wounds, the matter of your clothes is the next point of concern," she replied.

"I'm afraid there's little one can do to fix them."

"It wouldn't hurt to try."

Cedric hesitated before his hand went to the hem of his shirt.

"You don't have to take your shirt off," Anne spoke up, blushing due to the realization that he had misinterpreted her statement. "It is possible to mend clothing while it's being worn."

"I believe that's a sure way to get pricked by a needle," he replied in a skeptical tone.

"I shall refrain from injuring you further, I promise."

As soon as she said that, his body relaxed. Anne began mending the holes at the back of his shirt, her eyebrows furrowed in focus.

Cedric broke the silence. "Earlier, you asked if I would inform my family about today's events. Would you do the same?"

It didn't take long for her to have an answer. "As much as I'd like to share such news, I fear my aunt would merely weaponize it against me. My uncle would be afraid for my safety, which could result in him preventing me from returning here ever again."

He nodded in understanding. "I suppose that's a justifiable reason for holding such information back."

Anne frowned, failing to maneuver the needle in the proper manner. "It is, indeed—ow!"

"What is it?" Cedric asked, turning to her with concern.

"I pricked my finger."

"Is it bleeding?"

"No, thankfully," she replied, turning away and placing her mending tools and salve in her reticule. "I didn't pay enough attention during sewing classes. My lady's maid was the one who carried out my assignments to fool my tutor."

"As long as you have her, your clothing should remain in top condition," Cedric noted. He glanced down at his shirt distastefully. "I'll have to contend with changing outfits when I return home."

"I can't let you wander about like this," Anne protested. "Seeing as your clothing's impossible to fix, we'll have to replace it instead."

"You have work to do, and I'm not inclined to leave you here alone."

She placed the box of artifacts in a corner and picked up her reticule. "I have had enough activity for today."

He raised an eyebrow. "You intend on making your exit now?"

"I do, indeed. Now, let's get you a new pair of clothes."

They departed together and wasted no time boarding Cedric's waiting coach. It had been only a couple of hours since their arrival, but it felt like more. Her first day of work wasn't so bad, Anne mused. She would take on more responsibilities the following day to compensate for the lack of productivity today.

She turned to Cedric with an amused smile. "What would my uncle say if he saw you like this?"

He smirked and shook his head. "He'd think the archaeological site was a jungle of sorts and that I'd just finished battling a wild animal."

"He wouldn't be wrong. Climbing is a strenuous activity."

"Not if you grew up scaling hills and trees in the countryside."

"Is that what you did?"

He nodded. "There wasn't much else a restless young boy could do in the summertime."

"I'm glad that habit has proven valuable for you in adulthood," she admitted.

"So do I."

***

The coach stopped in front of a shop renowned for its sale of ready-made clothes. The fittings weren't always perfect, and their quality paled next to that of custom-made suits, but it would do for now.

Cedric stepped out and offered Anne his hand, which she took gratefully. For two individuals working together to further their respective interests, they got along relatively well.

She was not prone to panic, as proven when he climbed into a trench to rescue an injured man. Many upper-class women would consider the event frightening enough to affect their fragile sensibilities and drive them to tears.

But not Anne. She'd praised him for taking the initiative and kindly tended to his wounds. As things were, he couldn't have asked for a better person to embark on a fake courtship with.

As they stepped inside the building, a thin man with graying hair hurried toward them. "Good day, Lord Stonehaven. Is there anything you'd like, my lord?"

"A new pair of trousers, a tailcoat, and a waistcoat is all I need, Yancey."

Yancey nodded, gesturing toward the changing area. "That shall be arranged quickly, my lord."

Within a matter of minutes, Cedric was restored to looking like a distinguished gentleman again. He rejoined Anne, who was surveying some paintings in the corner while she waited for him.

"That didn't take long," she observed in a relieved tone, glancing sideways to look at him. "Shopping trips with my aunt are much worse. They involve walking from shop to shop for hours on end, deliberating about fabric and other irrelevant subjects. I much prefer shopping with Felicity over such humdrum."

"Mothers are fickle beings, far too exacting over little details," he replied sympathetically. "Not that I blame them for it. They tend to be on the receiving end of criticism when a child falls out of line."

"That may be true, but it doesn't make their haranguing any easier to bear."

"You're correct," Cedric said, thinking of his mother and her occasionally infuriating tendencies. "Yet, we love them for it."

Anne sighed. "I suppose I do not hate Bernice, although I must confess I find her personality grating."

Before he could say anything else, he heard his name being called.

"Lord Stonehaven," the voice repeated, clearly belonging to a woman. "Is that truly you?"

He turned to find a young lady staring at him expectantly. Instantly, he could tell she belonged to the category of women who liked him romantically. Unlike before, when he'd have felt obligated to converse or pretend to be interested to avoid offending her, he now had Anne as an excuse.

"Forgive me, madam, a truly fascinating sight captured my attention," he said, turning meaningfully to Anne. She slid her hand through his arm, her body warmth seeping distinctly through his clothes.

To the outside eye, they looked like two individuals enthralled with each other. Anne added more credibility to their act by glancing up semi-shyly at him, a move so convincing he wondered how long she'd spent practicing it.

"O-oh, I'm sorry to have interrupted you both. Goodbye!" The lady stammered out, her eyes growing wide before she hurried out of sight.

A relieved Cedric nodded in satisfaction. "This arrangement seems to be working perfectly."

"Not quite," Anne replied. "I barely did anything of value today. However, I can't wait to head home and have dinner."

Cedric chuckled. "For the sake of your productivity, I'll refrain from rash and potentially dangerous acts henceforth."

"I truly hope so."

They left the shop and boarded the carriage, the vehicle racing determinedly as he escorted her home.

Chapter Six

Cedric awoke to a persistent grating sound. He sat up in bed to find his cousin, Jasper, moving a wooden figurine back and forth across a table.

"It appears I've made more noise than I intended to," Jasper said in a tone that wasn't at all apologetic. "I had forgotten how much of a light sleeper you are."

His cousin had disappeared several months before without warning, nowhere to be found despite Cedric's relentless searching. It soon became apparent that he was hiding away on purpose, damning any concerns anyone might have held for him. To say his appearance now was sudden would be an understatement.

Cedric's eyes narrowed. "The question is, who let you in my room."

Jasper shrugged. "The maids let me in after repeatedly stating that you were asleep. I am family, after all."

"Rather unfortunately," Cedric murmured through gritted teeth. "For what reason have you so kindly bestowed me with your presence today?"

Jasper pointed at a cup of tea placed on the bedside table. "Your valet brought this in a few minutes before you woke up. I know how grumpy you can get without your morning tea."

Cedric reached for the tea and took several sips before refixing his gaze on his cousin. "Well?"

His cousin dragged a chair forward and sat opposite him. "I know you're upset by my actions, but I didn't choose to act that way irrationally."

"I invited you to watch one of my races. My thoroughbred won, only for you to claim the winning prize and disappear from sight."

Jasper raised his hands defensively. "You see, I needed the money urgently and—"

Cedric's glare remained unrelenting. "Not only that, I found out that your greed had led you to manipulate the race in my favor. You wanted the prize money of 10,000 pounds, so you threatened the judges and intimidated them into deciding the results before the race had even ended. Do you deny this?"

"I do not."

"What did you say to the judges to make them do your bidding?"

"I informed them that your father, the duke, was personally invested in seeing you win and that he'd reward them handsomely for rigging the results."

"I didn't ask you to do that," Cedric said firmly. "You fled with the prize money while I gained a scandalous reputation for influencing races in my favor."

"I had my reasons for acting in such a manner," Jasper replied stiffly.

Cedric folded his arms. "Now would be a good time to explain them."

"Weeks before you invited me to watch the race, I accumulated a hefty debt. I needed money to pay it off, but I had no available options for acquiring funds."

Cedric raised a disbelieving eyebrow. "To my knowledge, your father placed you on a monthly stipend of two thousand pounds when you turned eighteen."

"At the start of the year, my *father*," Jasper bit the word out with barely concealed resentment, "cut off my allowance as punishment for my decision to halt my studies."

"You dropped out of Eton?"

Jasper rolled his eyes. "I never could understand the appeal of long lectures and heavy books. I figured it would be best to explore a different way of life."

"By racking up debts?"

Jasper tapped his foot against the ground impatiently. "I invested in a business venture that imploded terribly. Such an outcome was unexpected but ultimately unavoidable, and it is therefore useless to blame myself."

"Perhaps so," Cedric responded.

Jasper sighed deeply and shot him an apologetic look. "I'm sorry for my actions and for the resulting consequences of my behavior. Truly, I had not expected the matter to blow up as it did. Luckily, the Steele family is influential enough not to be thoroughly affected by a scandal."

"A minor scandal," Cedric corrected. "I'm lucky that the rumors about me aren't widespread and that the few gentlemen privy to it view it as an interesting piece of information, not an outright confirmation of bad character. Still, that hasn't stopped me from being mocked and whispered about."

"My behavior was unbecoming of a cousin and gentleman," Jasper said, hanging his head sadly. "I hope to make amends somehow."

Never one to hold grudges for an extended time, Cedric's gaze softened. He and Jasper had grown up together, after all. Moreover, he was a valued family member.

"Consider the matter settled," he replied with a dismissive wave. "Now, let us move on to more compelling subjects."

There was a distinctive knock on the door, which Cedric quickly recognized as his mother's.

"Enter."

"Good morning, Cedric," his mother said, walking into the room. "Are you well-rested?"

"Good morning, Mother. I feel rejuvenated after a proper night's rest."

She turned to Jasper and observed him warily before saying in a deliberately polite tone, "Jasper, I didn't expect to find you here so early."

Jasper met her eyes with a sheepish smile. "I had an urgent matter to discuss with Cedric, Your Grace. Thankfully, Barnaby, your butler, was present to let me in."

"I see," his mother replied, a faint frown on her face. "I hope my sister is well. Has she returned to London?"

His cousin shifted in his seat uncomfortably before responding, "She is indeed, and sends her regards. She remains in Woolbridge for now, enjoying the cool countryside air and making changes around the manor."

His mother nodded, appeased by the answer. "Be sure to give her my love when you see her. I've been meaning to write, but your mother is the sort to delay reading her letters, and I find waiting long for a response rather tedious."

Jasper chuckled, although it came out more like a broken sound. "Very well. I shall convey your regards at my earliest convenience."

"Given that you will not be present for dinner, make sure to eat something filling for lunch," she said, returning her attention to Cedric.

"I shall endeavor to," he replied.

She nodded her approval and made toward the door. "That's all I wanted to say to you."

Jasper cast an accusatory glance at Cedric after his mother's departure. "You neglected to mention that you were headed somewhere."

"I wasn't aware that I needed to report my whereabouts to you for input," Cedric replied coolly.

"I would simply like to know."

"And I would like to refrain from speaking about it."

"It wouldn't hurt to share," Jasper pressed.

Cedric sighed. "I shall be attending a popular race in Epsom later this afternoon."

"By yourself?"

"I'll have my valet accompany me."

"He's your staff," his cousin said with a roll of his eyes. "He'll be present because you pay him to. You'll lack good company and excellent conversation during your trip."

"Epsom's only a short carriage ride away. I'm certain I shall manage excellently."

"Hiding away for so long has left me with an appetite for company and travel. A trip such as this is precisely what I need."

Cedric rose from his bed and rang the bell for valet. A warm tub of water and some minutes spent shaving were all he needed to start his day. While he waited for his valet to arrive, he turned to his cousin.

"You can join me on the trip to Epsom," he said finally. "However, you'll have to promise not to bet on any horses or attempt to influence race outcomes."

Jasper nodded. "I promise."

Smith, his valet, appeared in the doorway. "Your bath is ready, my lord, and your carriage has been prepared for immediate usage."

"Thank you, Smith," Cedric said.

"Are you headed someplace this morning?"

"When did you get into the habit of asking numerous questions?"

Jasper shrugged. "A lot seems to have happened in my absence. I would like to fill in the gaps."

"If you must know, I've been courting a woman," Cedric began with some hesitation. He contemplated whether to tell Jasper the truth, then decided against it. Secrets were better kept the fewer people knew about them.

Instead, he shared the details of Anne's employment and his role in accompanying her to work.

"I'm happy for you, cousin," Jasper said, slapping him on his back.

"Now that that's settled, will you leave while I prepare for the day?"

"Certainly," Jasper replied with a mock salute before leaving the room.

***

Anne leaned comfortably against the plush carriage seat and flipped through the pages of her book. Her reading was unhampered by the moving vehicle, and she felt refreshed after a good night's rest.

Cedric had arrived on time to pick her up, and that was hugely relieving, given that she planned to get more work done today. He sat opposite her, a man with a strong physical presence that was both striking and calming.

She would have to pay immense attention to the artifacts when examining them, Anne thought. Regardless of whether they were real or fake, it was likely they would yield information in relation to their history and origin.

If the artifacts did turn out to be fake, they would be abandoned for other projects. But if they were confirmed to be authentic, the items would be delivered to museums for safekeeping.

"I hate to interrupt your reading," Cedric said, pulling her from her thoughts. "What book is that?"

She blinked, surprised by his interest. "It's titled *Weaponry Artifact Research*, and I got it from my father's library. It will assist me in determining the origin and purpose of some of the items."

"How, specifically?"

"It's a complicated process, and I don't wish to bore you—"

"I assure you I'd like to know all about it."

It was clear that the weaponry aspect of the title had piqued his attention. Anne adjusted in her seat, eager to answer his question. "The quality of the material and craftsmanship can offer clues about the historical nature of the items. For example, bronze statues and weapons were used by the Romans and Celtics, while crucifixes and chalices are more likely to be from the Medieval period. Do you understand?"

Cedric stroked his chin, digesting the new information. "Can you precisely determine how old an arrow or bow artifact could be?"

"Unfortunately not," Anne said. "For now, I and others in this field can only make educated guesses. I believe someday humans will invent equipment to determine that accurately."

"It's interesting that humans dueled with items of all shapes and sizes."

"The Celts were famous for using fast chariots with deadly scythe blades attached to the wheels for mowing down enemies."

His eyes widened. "Truly?"

"That's mild when compared to other savage weapons in history."

Cedric leaned forward in his seat. "Tell me more."

Anne did as he asked, regaling him with tales of lesser-known figures in history and their feats in battle. Cedric listened with rapt attention as they descended the carriage, walked through the gates leading to the dig, and made for her office.

"I'm relieved to know I haven't bored you," She finished, settling behind her desk.

"The entire conversation was quite illuminating," he replied, settling in his assigned seat. "I did not expect to enjoy discussing history so much."

They settled into an easy silence, only occasionally punctuated by Cedric flipping through the pages of his book about horses. Anne's first task was to write a letter to Mr. Nigel thanking him for encouraging her to pursue her aspirations. She told him about the presumed fakeness of the artifacts discovered at the dig and assured him that she would continue researching.

Next, Anne spread the artifacts out on her desk and thoroughly examined each item. It was the preliminary round of inspections, and she scribbled new theories and discoveries in her pocketbook.

As she worked, it occurred to her that Cedric didn't seem to underestimate her work. He granted her needed silence and read his book instead.

She was, therefore, surprised when he rose from his seat and stepped out of the office. A minute later, he returned with a wicker basket.

"You're due for a lunch break," he said, retrieving two metal containers from the basket and placing one on her table. "I asked my cook to make us lunch every afternoon for a groom to deliver."

"Thank you," Anne replied, hesitant to leave her task.

"You should eat, Anne," Cedric urged firmly. "That way, you'll be refreshed and ready to take on more tasks."

"I suppose I could take a brief break," she said, blushing slightly when her stomach grumbled hungrily in agreement. She sat down and picked up her fork, touched by his kind gesture.

"I wasn't sure which flavors you prefer, so I asked the cook to include a variety of meals," he explained.

She opened the container to find slices of meat, cheese, bread, pastries, and fruit. "This is a lovely spread. While we eat, would you like to share how you became interested in horse breeding?"

Her aunt had always disapproved of speaking while at the dining table, but Anne had never listened. Besides, there were no dining tables present and, by extension, no need to uphold such a rule.

Cedric chewed thoughtfully and swallowed before replying, "I always liked horses growing up, and when I was old enough, I decided I wanted to be involved in breeding the best horses in England."

"Was it difficult to set up your stud farm?"

"Not particularly," he replied with a shake of his head. "My father granted me permission to transform a block of inns in his ownership into a stud farm. Breeding and sorting out the horses was more difficult, but thanks to a capable training staff and hard work on my part, I overcame harsh obstacles. Now, I no longer need to visit the farm daily and rest knowing my horses are in safe hands."

"The next time I attend a race, I'll be sure to keep an eye out for horses your farm raised."

Cedric chuckled. "That's a brilliant idea, and I'm certain you will not be disappointed."

"Perhaps one day, you'll show me around the farm," Anne said.

"I'm afraid it's no place for a lady," he replied regretfully. "But I might let you visit if you promise not to stray out of sight."

"I promise."

"We shall have to depart early today," Cedric said apologetically. "There's a racing event in Epsom that requires my attention."

"That's alright," Anne responded. "I'm nearly through with my tasks for the day. What will you do when my employment is over, and our false courtship comes to an end?"

"I shall depart to Devonshire to spend time with my father," Cedric shared, wiping his mouth with a napkin. "How about you?"

"I'll return to my interests and resume a tiring cycle of attending balls," she answered, stating the last part of her sentence with a frustrated groan. "Believe me, I can't wait till I turn 21 and receive my inheritance. I turned 20 recently; therefore, I've got a year's worth of waiting left."

Cedric shook his head sympathetically. "The wait sounds bleak. We may as well enjoy our meals and appreciate the bliss-filled present."

Anne smiled. "That may be the best advice I have received in a long while."

As they dug into their meals, Anne decided Cedric was a unique gentleman with admirable traits.

Chapter Seven

The afternoon sun in Epsom rose high in the sky, illuminating the racecourse with a golden glow. The air buzzed with excitement as spectators gathered beneath grandstands, their hats and bonnets arrayed in an almost decorative pattern.

"Which one's yours?" Jasper asked, straining forward to view the cleared field better.

"Number four," Cedric replied. "He's an Arabian thoroughbred with top speed and stamina, ridden by a talented jockey I'm lucky to have in my employ."

"He looks magnificent."

"I am in agreement with that statement," Cedric said with a brief nod. "If the Arabian does well, I expect to have a flood of sales soon."

A hush descended over the crowd at the sound of a blaring trumpet. Everyone watched with rapt attention as the horses darted past the starting gates, raising a cloud of dust behind them. The jockeys rode expertly, urging their steeds forward through a combination of body language, encouraging shouts, and skilled maneuvering.

Each time a horse was overtaken by another, there were triumphant cheers or disappointed groans in the stands. The lead changed several times, leaving the audience ever more invested as they sat on the edge of their seats.

Cedric's focus didn't waver from the Arabian. The horse was fast, and there was a fluidity to his movement that made the distance easy to conquer. He was neck to neck with another horse, a Turk with powerful hind legs. Neither seemed willing to give their position as the race drew toward the final stretch.

The atmosphere was replete with thundering hooves as the jockeys urged their mounts forward with every bit of their strength. With a final burst of speed, the Turk crossed the finish line, the Arabian trailing after him a few seconds later.

Cedric was pleased by his horse's performance. The Arabian had come in second place, which was an achievement in itself. With a little more training, there was a good chance he would win the next race he ran.

Congratulatory messages were exchanged, and winning prizes were handed out. Cedric and Jasper returned to their carriage as it set off toward London.

"What's the prize amount for coming in second place?"

"Fifteen thousand pounds," Cedric replied. The money was sitting comfortably in his money belt.

"May I have it?" Jasper asked. "Such a sum would be beneficial to me, dear cousin. You, on the other hand, do not really need the money."

Cedric tossed the money belt to him. "You can have it. Winning horse races is good for business, which is why I participate. The prize money is of little importance."

Jasper grinned. "Remind me to join you in attending similar races."

"Somehow, I doubt you'll be present for much longer."

"Are you accusing me of planning to disappear again?" his cousin said, placing a dramatic hand over his chest. "I'll have you know that was a one-time incident."

Cedric glanced at him skeptically. "I suppose we'll see how everything plays out."

"I won't disappear, and if I decide to leave London, I shall notify you first," Jasper replied cheerfully, securing the money belt underneath his clothes. "What do you feel for Lady Anne?"

Cedric tapped his fingers against his temple, thoughts forming about the said woman. Anne was always a beautiful woman, but the little details about her had caught his attention more.

He enjoyed her animated approach to narrating historical facts and the slight furrow of her eyebrows whenever she was immersed in work. Lately, she'd begun to strike his interest more.

"She's a special woman whom I'm beginning to grow fond of," he admitted hesitantly. "But only platonically."

"Platonically?"

Drat. He had forgotten to play the role of the enamored suitor. His cousin was one of his closest friends, which explained his initial instinct to reply honestly.

He may as well go all the way, Cedric decided. He informed Jasper about the entire truth of his arrangement with Anne, and his cousin's eyes widened in surprise.

"That's quite a drastic decision."

"It is," Cedric agreed. "However, it was the only way I could be rid of my mother's nagging."

"It seems like a more strenuous alternative," Jasper pointed out. "Now you have significantly less time to yourself, given that you've been tasked with accompanying her to work."

Cedric leaned back in his seat. "It isn't so terrible. Lady Anne is an admirable woman who is both intelligent and well-mannered."

"That's more than I have heard you say about any other lady."

"I pride myself on being a good judge of character."

"What does Lady Anne do at the dig? Other than sit around and look pretty?"

"Don't say that," Cedric retorted, unable to help the rising irritation caused by his cousin's disregarding tone. "She analyzes the discovered items and draws conclusions based on them."

"Such as?"

"The period of creation and usage. Whether they are real or fake alongside other details."

"What happens when the items are determined to be real?"

Cedric cast a sideway glance at Jasper. "I didn't know you had such an avid interest in archaeology."

Jasper shrugged and stared out the window. "There are a lot of things you don't know about me."

***

After a thoroughly refreshing nap, Anne reached for her pocketbook and read through her observations. She had already determined the period and purpose of the items, although further research would be required before drafting her final conclusion.

She had accomplished a lot with only a day's work, Anne thought proudly, setting the pocketbook on her bedside table.

Mr. Nigel and The Society of Antiquaries of London would have little choice but to assign her more jobs by the time she sent them her well-researched findings.

It was considered crass by some to bring work home, but not Anne. She went to her writing desk and began poring through a book about historical materials. It would aid her in her next task of determining whether the items at the dig were real or fake.

A knock on the door interrupted her focus.

"Enter."

Polly walked in, her eyebrow raising slightly at the sight of Anne at the desk. "If I recall correctly, you informed me you were going to nap."

"I did nap," Anne replied. "Then I woke up and decided it would be best to work some more."

Polly nodded, appeased by the reply. "As your lady's maid, my priority is that you do not overwork yourself."

"I know, Polly," she replied, smiling in appreciation. "And I'm grateful to you for that."

"I have good news. Lady Felicity has returned from her honeymoon."

Anne drew her chair back and leapt to her feet. "Truly?"

Polly picked a piece of clothing from the floor and tucked it into a drawer. "I wouldn't jest over such a topic. I know how much you've pined for her return."

"I must visit at once. I'm certain Felicity would not mind me dropping by without a prior message."

Polly moved over to the armoire and retrieved a muslin gown. "In that case, we'd best get you dressed."

A couple of minutes later, a properly dressed Anne emerged from the house and boarded her coach. The journey to Felicity's home was brief and replete with excitement. As the four-wheeled vehicle raced along the smooth road, her nerves thrummed in anticipation of seeing her cousin again.

Although Felicity was a year older, they had been inseparable for most of their lives. Anne would have hardly managed the loss of her parents if Felicity hadn't been present to provide comfort and needed humor. Similarly, Felicity's spirited personality would have gone unappreciated if Anne hadn't provided support and praise for it.

Anne's coach drew to a stop in front of a brown townhouse with a stucco facade. It was occupied by the Montgomery household, and Felicity, who had married Lord Sheffield, who was the first son of the family, now lived there.

A footman opened the door and helped her out. She approached the main entrance just as the main door drew open, and the butler smiled warmly.

"Good afternoon, my lady. I presume you're here to see Lady Sheffield."

"You're correct, Higgins. I hope to see my cousin again after two weeks of absence," Anne replied, climbing up the polished stairs and into the house. "Will you kindly inform her of my presence?"

"Certainly," Higgins replied. "You can settle comfortably in the parlor, my lady."

He bowed respectfully before walking away. Through the years, Anne had paid the townhouse many visits, mainly to see her friend Marie Montgomery. They were of similar ages. A few months ago, Marie had fallen in love with a wealthy American businessman whom she married and now lived with in Boston.

Anne was happy for her friend and for Felicity, whose antagonistic attitude toward Colin Montgomery had been interesting to watch until the two fell madly in love.

She decided against going to the parlor. Her excitement was simply too great to sit and drink tea. Instead, she stood in the grand hall, which allowed her a good glimpse of her cousin as she approached.

It almost seemed implausible that Felicity, a golden-haired beauty with high cheekbones, heart-shaped lips, and a mischievous smile, would grow even prettier, but that was precisely what looked to have occurred.

Her porcelain skin glowed with health and a little bit of something else. Contentment, Anne guessed, and bliss from being profusely loved.

"My darling Anne!" Felicity exclaimed in her signature high voice, pulling her into a warm embrace. "Gorgeous as always. I have missed you terribly."

"Believe me, I have missed you more," Anne replied as they separated.

"How many letters did you write and successfully send off?" Felicity asked in a half-playful, half-challenging tone.

"Six letters in total, but I'm doubtful you received any of them."

"You win," her cousin replied, taking her hand and walking in the direction of the parlor. "I wrote three letters and got two delivered. Our seaside resort in Brighton had incredible views that were simply too good to pass on, so Colin and I extended our stay by a few more days."

"That would explain why I sent a letter to an inn I was certain you'd stop at to no avail."

Felicity raised an eyebrow. "Were you truly that desperate to talk to me?"

"I was," Anne admitted. "A lot has occurred in my life since you left for your honeymoon."

"Positive or negative?"

"Positive," she confirmed. "Although at first, I wasn't certain how well things would turn out."

The parlor was decorated differently from when she had last visited. Silk wallpaper lined the walls, a plush crimson carpet covered the wooden floorboards, and the armchairs were upholstered in flowery brocade.

"My mother-in-law made a few changes around the house in celebration of our marriage," Felicity explained as if reading her mind.

"How's Lady Sheffield?"

"She's out calling on friends," her cousin replied.

A maid brought in a cup of tea and set it on a table opposite Anne. "And your husband?"

"He's busy sorting out his pile of unread letters. He'll join us shortly," Felicity said, drawing closer. "Now tell me everything. I'm all ears."

"It all began when I received a letter from Mr. Nigel, offering employment at an archaeological dig."

"Oh Anne," Felicity exclaimed, hugging her briefly. "I'm so happy for you."

"Thank you," replied Anne, pleased by her cousin's enthusiasm. "Your aunt wasn't as pleased by the news."

Felicity rolled her eyes. "Bernice's opinion is not to be taken seriously."

"In any case, she tried to convince your father that working at the dig would be a waste of time," Anne continued, sipping her tea. "That failed, by the way. He decided instead to grant me permission to resume at the dig if I met one condition."

"What was it?"

"I had to find a respectable suitor willing to accompany me to the dig through the course of my employment and keep me safe."

"How ridiculous," Felicity said sharply. "Does he think suitors of that sort fall in droves from the sky? It's a nearly impossible task."

Anne smiled triumphantly. "Anyway, I achieved it."

Felicity's eyes glinted with interest. "How?"

Anne explained how she'd written a letter to Felicity, only for it to be misdelivered to Cedric. She then went on to narrate everything else that had occurred. The room descended into silence once she stopped talking as Felicity digested the new information.

Her cousin finally spoke. "Do you find Lord Stonehaven to be a respectable gentleman?"

"I do. He's quite easy to get along with and rather nice too, although his bluntness could rub others the wrong way."

"But not you?"

"Not me," Anne responded. "I find his bluntness somewhat interesting."

"How fascinating."

The manner in which Felicity dragged the words out spoke to an unrevealed sentiment, but before Anne could question her further, someone walked in.

The unmistakable broad figure of Colin Montgomery approached them. Like Felicity, he looked satisfied and perfectly at peace with life. His sun-kissed hair, which used to be typically combed down, was slightly in disarray, signaling a more carefree side of him.

"I have successfully sorted out two weeks' worth of correspondence, which makes me rather fulfilled," He announced, settling in an armchair beside his wife. "It's good to see you again, Anne. I trust you've been well?"

"As well as anyone possibly can be in London," Anne answered.

"Your valet would have handled that task just as well," Felicity pointed out, wiping a smudge of dust on his face with her thumb.

Colin leaned over and kissed her forehead. "I'm far too meticulous to pass up the chance to sort my letters, and you know it."

"Thankfully, I enjoy your assiduous nature, otherwise it would be mind-boggling."

Colin chuckled. "That, my dear, is why we're married now and no longer at each other's throats." He rose to his feet and adjusted his tailcoat. "I'm afraid I must take my leave for a little while. I promised Alexander I'd visit him upon my return. Will you be terribly lonely in my absence?"

"Not particularly, although I'd love it if you could be present for dinner," Felicity answered.

"I wouldn't miss it for the world," Colin promised, leaning to press another kiss on her forehead.

As Anne observed their exchange, she felt an unusual tinge rising in her chest. It was unfamiliar, so she concluded it was a feeling of joy toward Felicity and Colin.

Once Colin departed, her cousin cleared her throat. "I paused my matchmaking venture due to the honeymoon, and now I'm ready to resume. This time, I'd like to take on personal projects."

Anne's eyes narrowed in suspicion. "I hope this doesn't mean you'll occupy yourself with finding me a match."

Felicity attempted to look innocent. "Personal projects can include a variety of meanings."

"I haven't found the right man, and I'm not opposed to doing so myself," Anne insisted. "I don't need extra help."

"You've gotten your point across, darling cousin," Felicity said. "Now let me tell you about the interesting sights I witnessed during my honeymoon."

Chapter Eight

Felicity Montgomery was a woman not easily dissuaded, especially when she had a stirring hunch about two potentially compatible individuals. However, she had made a promise to her sweet cousin Anne, vowing to refrain from interfering in her personal affairs. Such an endeavor was easier said than done, but Felicity was determined to try.

A woman having her own study was unconventional in London society, but Felicity had always been provided access to one. First in her father's household and now in her husband's.

It was where she worked most days, sorting out files and requests from people—men and women who wished to be matched with someone who shared the language of their heart. There were lots of successful matches and little to no failures, which made Felicity an expert in her field.

Her keen sense and wit were ample tools for an excellent matchmaking career. Felicity often relied on a mix of fact and instinct, although some could describe her methods as unorthodox.

She glanced out the window and tapped her fingers against the large mahogany desk. Halfway through her cousin's narration the previous day, she had sensed a budding connection between Anne and Lord Stonehaven.

Would she dare to renege on her earlier promise to Anne for the chance that her instincts were correct?

Before Felicity could decide on an answer, Johanna, her friend and assistant, walked into the study. She was a sweet-faced woman with curly brown hair and paid precise attention to detail. Like Felicity, she was born to a distinguished English family but found other interests more compelling than balls and soirées.

"I found a pocketbook in the parlor," she announced. "It seems to be Anne's."

"It must have fallen from her reticule," Felicity held out her hand. "I'll give it to her when I go visiting."

Johanna blushed. "I wasn't snooping by any means. I simply found the book open next to an armchair, so I took a look at the page."

"What did you find?" Felicity asked curiously.

"Perhaps it would be best if you read it yourself."

Johanna handed her the pocketbook. Along a page, Anne had written a list of traits she liked in a man. *Someone who accepts and tolerates her hobbies, is honorable, considerate...*

A bell rang in Felicity's head as she set the book down. Those traits aligned with what Anne had told her regarding Lord Stonehaven. For Anne's sake, she needed to interfere and help provide her cousin a chance at happiness.

"Johanna, I'd like you to take on an urgent task."

"Certainly. Just tell me what it is."

"Look into Lord Stonehaven and submit any new information to me as soon as possible."

Johanna nodded and walked toward the door. "I shall get started right away."

Felicity tapped her fingers against the desk again. She was certain something romantic could occur between the earl and her cousin.

***

Anne's focus was unwavering as she thoroughly examined the artifacts on her desk. She analyzed each piece individually, taking care to hold it carefully to avoid scratches and inadvertent breakage.

The Roman ring was heavy and carved with an inscription that translated to 'live, we shall.' The intricate cut and styling were too distinct to be forged; moreover, the little cracks along the band spoke to an organic and gradual passage of time.

It wasn't a fake, that much was for certain. The ring likely once sat around the finger of a wealthy businessman during the period when Rome occupied England.

She moved on to the spearheads and figurines, which were highly detailed and clearly molded by intelligent minds. A replica would be incapable of exuding as much dignified authority. She observed the details—the sharp end of authentic steel, dried blood from battle, and chiseled faces. Her knowledge of history helped her place them as originating from the Medieval Age.

As she worked, a sense of satisfaction bloomed within her. The process of checking each item and documenting accurate conclusions brought her much joy. This was beyond reading books in the library; it was about handling first-hand historical evidence and shedding light on the past.

"The artifacts aren't fake after all," Anne announced in amazement, breaking the silence.

"Truly?" Cedric asked, setting his book and walking over to her desk.

She nodded, picking up the ring and tapping her fingers thoughtfully against it. "In addition, these pieces are sturdy, not fragile and unremarkable as Hatter presented them to be."

"Perhaps they threw out the broken items, and these are all that's left."

Anne pursed her lips doubtfully. "I believe Hatter wouldn't neglect to mention that important detail. These may be all the pieces discovered, but the men seem to hold an inaccurate opinion of them."

"Do you think Hatter and the others were being genuine in their statements?"

Anne furrowed her eyebrows. "I'm not certain."

"I'm inclined to think they were," Cedric replied.

"Why is that the case?"

"Many of these men are uneducated, and their skill set lies in digging holes and trenches. Their conclusion that the artifacts are fake isn't from a nuanced perspective."

"You mean their claims are unfounded?"

"Precisely," he answered. "Their strong belief that the artifacts are fake must have come from someone else."

"What sort of individual would spread such a rumor?"

Cedric snapped his fingers. "Someone with an unknown motive, whom the men trusted enough to believe his or her words."

"Owners of properties where historical items are discovered tend to be protective of their land," Anne said. "Maybe the owner of this land spread lies about the falseness of the items to dissuade researchers like myself from prying."

"That may be the case," he replied. "Do you know how your employers gained permission to be on this land in the first place?"

"The discovery of a historical site made it into the newspaper, which is how the Society of Antiquaries of London came to know about it. Maybe the owner felt compelled to appease the curious public, but only for a little while."

"That's likely, but we can't know for certain until a proper investigation has been conducted," Cedric stated.

Anne released an awed sigh. "I can't believe I was able to confirm the authenticity of the items."

She felt Cedric's reassuring hand on her shoulder. "You did an incredible job, providing clarity where previously there was doubt. Congratulations on your discovery."

"Thank you, kindly. Your words are most gracious," she replied, glowing in appreciation. She wasn't sure which she liked better—his compliments or whenever he gave her his full attention.

"Some would say you've achieved a feat almost as great as Boudicca, Queen of the Iceni tribe," he said, smiling.

"No one could ever compare to that fierce woman."

"But one can certainly try," Cedric finished. He was beginning to pick up on her historical knowledge, which made their conversations far richer.

Anne sat behind her desk and picked up her quill pen. "I shall write a letter to Mr. Nigel at once, informing him of my discoveries thus far."

Cedric nodded and picked up his book. "I, on the other hand, shall provide the quiet you need."

The afternoon sun cast a warm glow across her desk as she dipped her quill pen into an inkwell and began writing to Mr. Nigel. She provided a complete recount of her research process and requested advice on the next steps to take.

"I'm all done," she announced shortly after. "This is a good time to head home for some rest."

"In my household, winning moments such as this one are celebrated with a gift," Cedric said, fixing her a smile. "Would you like to stop by a bookstore with me?"

Anne blinked in surprise. "You wish to buy me a book?"

"I thought long and hard about it before concluding a book would please you best. Or would you prefer a different gift?"

"A book would be perfect, thank you."

"Then we'd best be on our way," Cedric replied, rising from his seat. "There's a bookstore further along the street, so we have no need for a carriage. It's only a few minutes away on foot."

"I like walking," she said out loud, picking up her reticule. "Although my uncle would much prefer I did that in the garden or at the park."

"He's right. The streets of London are not safe for young ladies, especially ones who come from moneyed families."

They exited the office and strolled along the pavement. Gentlemen and ladies hurried about with their valets or lady's maids following closely while carriages and hackneys raced by at a quick speed.

Although Anne did not care for balls and other events of the Season, she enjoyed London for its cool ambiance and easier accessibility to essential things like books and tools.

"Sadly, the subject of potential harm is one unmoneyed ladies suffer under as well," she said, continuing their conversation. "Perhaps one day, ladies from various backgrounds will be able to walk the streets freely without fear."

"I strongly hope that such a day will come," Cedric replied.

They stopped in front of a building with brown walls and a door distinctly painted blue. A large signboard with the words 'Aggy's Bookstore' served as an identifier.

As they entered, Anne took in the lovely sight of leather-bound books spanning various topics. The store would never compare to the library left behind by her parents, but it still made for an intriguing sight.

"There are so many options to choose from," Anne remarked happily.

"What type of book interests you?"

"I've been meaning to acquire the latest edition of *The Egyptian Historian* by Matthew Hallway. I wonder if I'll find it here."

"Do you have it?" Cedric asked, turning to the bookkeeper, a white-haired man with a pair of spectacles that sat high on his nose.

"I do, indeed. I shall bring it to you, if you would so kindly give me a moment," the man replied, hurrying toward the back of the store to fetch the aforementioned item.

"I'd like to buy you a book, too," Anne said, whirling around to face him fully. Until now, she'd never quite realized how nicely his gray eyes fit within his face. It made for an undoubtedly pleasant sight.

"You don't have to. This is a gift for you, not the other way around."

"I want to," she insisted. "Better still, let us exchange books based on the other's interests. You'll take *The Egyptian Historian* while I take a book you prefer."

"A brilliant idea," Cedric replied. "In that case, I'd like to recommend *Navigating the Horses Upbringing*, a book by the renowned specialist Alexander Gardener."

Anne smiled. "I look forward to reading it and learning more about why the topic intrigues you."

Cedric returned her smile. "I feel the same way. I suspect *The Egyptian History* will keep me occupied in the following days."

She had never been the sort of person to classify her life in terms of good or bad days. But as Anne stood in the bookstore with Cedric, she couldn't help thinking that the day was ending on an excellent note.

Chapter Nine

Felicity was sorting through a pile of matchmaking requests when Johanna walked into the study with a triumphant smile.

"I did as you asked, and I'm pleased to report that I have valuable information about Lord Stonehaven," she said, taking the seat opposite Felicity. "I could get used to enquiring about lords and their counterparts. You would be surprised by how willing people are to gossip about titled individuals."

Felicity wrinkled her nose. "I can't say I am. Growing up in the ton has revealed to me that it's a breeding ground for recycled stories and unpleasant exchanges."

"I spent most of my life in the countryside, never visiting London until the previous year, so it's all still new to me," Johanna murmured, glancing down at her fingers.

"And yet you've managed to build valuable connections with a special knack for collecting information."

Johanna laughed humorlessly. "That's only because no one considers me of much importance. They interact with me because I'm the daughter of a duke, and they hope to gain his favor."

Felicity reached over to hold her friend's hand. "You're not unimportant, and if anyone dares say that to me, they'll have a huge problem on their hands. I value you both as a friend and an assistant, do you understand?"

Johanna nodded, a smile spreading across her face. "Only a fool would dare cross you."

Felicity observed her friend quietly. Early in the matchmaking venture, she'd vowed to refrain from interfering in the love lives of individuals she knew personally. That decision had been borne out of her lack of desire to blur the lines between work and life. Lately, she was beginning to waver on that principle.

Her loved ones also deserved to find fulfillment, even if it came about due to Felicity's direct involvement.

She leaned closer. "Darling Jo, are you unhappy?"

"I know that look. You're considering taking me on as your next project after Anne."

"Do you object to that?"

"I have no use for romantic love, which is rather ironic given my present occupation," Johanna remarked, waving her hand in a dismissive gesture. "Let us speak instead about Lord Stonehaven."

"The discussion isn't over yet," Felicity warned, setting the pile of papers aside. "But I'm willing to let myself be distracted this one time."

"In addition to my personal inquiry, I hired an investigator to gather information about the earl," Johanna paused to tuck a strand of hair behind her ear before continuing. "He seems to be a respectable gentleman from a revered household, except for a minor scandal that occurred months ago."

Felicity perked up with interest. "What scandal?"

"According to a trusted source, he and his cousin manipulated the results of a racing event so his horse could win."

"He breeds racehorses?" Felicity questioned, raising an eyebrow.

"Yes, and he seems to have had a successful run thus far," Johanna remarked. "His horses are highly sought after, known to come either first or second place in a race."

"Do you have any other less than pleasant news about him?"

"There's none. He has no unresolved feuds or notable enemies and is rather known for his easygoing personality."

Felicity tilted her head thoughtfully. "That means he's unlikely to be a greedy horse breeder. In all likelihood, the scandal involving him may well be a misunderstanding."

"I agree," Johanna replied. "I have the feeling Lord Stonehaven will make a fine husband someday."

"With any luck, that lady will be Anne," Felicity said, sorting through her desk for unused papers. She picked up a quill and thrust it toward Johanna. "I need you to write two letters signed by Anne and Cedric, respectively, inviting each other to a ball."

***

Anne sat at her desk and flipped through the pages of a book about ancient civilizations. The night sky peeked through her window, highlighted by sparkling stars and ink-blue clouds.

She had managed to resist her aunt's persistent urgings to attend a prestigious ball occurring tonight. That was a huge achievement, given Bernice's tenacious spirit. Her cousins, however, hadn't been so lucky. Tessa and Alix were likely downstairs now, being harried by

Bernice as she fussed over the little details of their gowns, hats, and other accessories.

Anne, on the other hand, was only too pleased to enjoy a peaceful night spent reading books and pondering over her discoveries thus far.

Now that it had been established that the artifacts were real, she planned to conduct more research while awaiting Mr. Nigel's reply. With any hope, the artifacts would be taken to a museum where they rightfully belonged.

A knock on the door and an answering response from Anne preceded Polly's entry.

"I've come to pick out your gown for tomorrow," her lady's maid said, walking over to the armoire and sifting through the clothes. "What fabric do you prefer? Muslin or chiffon?"

"It's a free day tomorrow, so there's no need for that," Anne replied, running her fingers through a strand of her hair. "I've had an interesting week so far."

"You undoubtedly enjoy being employed," Polly observed with a kind smile. "What's your favorite aspect of working?"

"I like leaving home to work on important projects. I like knowing my contributions are valued and useful to society."

Her lady's maid raised an eyebrow. "Is that all?"

"Were you hoping to hear something else?"

"I was, actually," Polly replied. She drew closer and sat on a nearby chair. "Have you enjoyed being around Lord Stonehaven these past few days?"

Anne picked up her quill pen and twirled it about. "I assure you, I have. I had hoped he'd make my time at the dig more enjoyable, and I'm relieved that has been the case."

"I'm glad you find his personality agreeable," Polly said. "I was worried that you two would find yourselves at loggerheads."

"Why is that the case?"

Polly lifted her shoulder in a shrug. "Not a lot of gentlemen hold generous views of a lady's interests. Most are too pompous and self-important to tolerate being around an intelligent and driven woman like yourself."

"I have witnessed that one too many times," Anne said, recalling a couple of instances when she'd been firmly rebuffed by gentlemen who preferred hearing their own voices instead.

"It's a wonder you didn't push back and give them a piece of your mind."

"Doing so would be scandalous, as Bernice says. Moreover, I consider myself above the petty politics of the ton."

Polly clucked her tongue sympathetically. "If your aim is to have a low profile within society, I'm afraid gaining employment was the wrong way to go."

"Luckily, the rewards of my decision have proven greater than the punishments," Anne replied. "Working at the dig has made me a very happy woman."

"I suggest you purchase a gift for Lord Stonehaven when the arrangement comes to an end."

For some unknown reason, Anne felt a pang in her heart at the thought of that. She had grown accustomed to spending long hours with him, and it would be incredibly lonely to return to her previous life.

"I have every intention of doing so," she answered. "It's the least I can do to thank him for the support."

Polly nodded in agreement. "It would be a nice gesture, indeed."

A knock on the door halted their conversation.

"Come in," Anne said.

A maid walked into the room, averting her eyes shyly as she drew closer. "There's a letter for you, my lady."

Anne raised a curious eyebrow as she took the letter and dismissed the maid. She scanned the paper, unable to keep a look of surprise from crossing her face as she read.

Dear Anne,

I hope this letter finds you well. A grand ball is to be held this evening at the Palmerston House. I'm certain you've heard about it, although the question as to whether you'll be present or not is yet to be concluded.

Given that, I would be honored if you would consider gracing the event with your presence. My attendance at the ball would be significantly improved with you around.

Yours sincerely,

Cedric Steele

Anne found it unusual that Cedric had written to her instead of discussing the topic physically during their last encounter. However, it was slightly flattering that he appreciated her company and was requesting more of it.

It was also normal for her to feel such immense joy, she told herself. After all, she had grown attached to him, understandably, since they'd been spending so much time together.

A thrum of excitement spread through Anne as she rose from her seat.

In reply to Polly's questioning look, she said simply, "It appears I will not be spending the evening at home after all."

A couple of minutes later, Anne headed downstairs and made in the direction of the drawing room. Her cousins were distinctly garbed in fashionable, expensive gowns, and their faces were dabbed with powder and rouge.

Tessa sat at the pianoforte, playing a melancholic tune, while Alix sipped her evening tea with a bored look on her face. The two glanced up at her entry.

"There's the lucky one," Tessa said, spinning around to look at her. "Have you come to wave your victory in our faces?"

"What victory?" Anne asked.

"The one over our stepmother, of course," Alix replied dryly. "You've been granted leave to spend your evening however you wish, whereas Tessa and myself have little choice but to contend with endless dances and futile conversation."

"I don't mind the festivities and dancing," Tessa admitted. "But I'd enjoy these events a lot more if Bernice weren't present."

"She schemes to marry us off, but her desperate attempts have only resulted in scaring potential suitors. No one wants to be hounded severally to dance with a lady," Alix commented, examining her nails. "Left to me, I'd rather be married to an—"

"American," Anne and Tessa finished with knowing grins.

"Your obsession with them astounds us all," Tessa added.

Alix looked puzzled, and her face glowed red. "I didn't realize I was talking about it constantly. Was I truly so obvious?"

"Do not stifle your interests on our account," Anne responded with a swift gesture of encouragement. "Feel free to dwell upon whatever group of people intrigue you."

"I am in agreement with that opinion," Tessa said, tapping a key on the pianoforte for emphasis. "Unless the group includes dangerous criminals, in which case I'll have little choice but to object."

"That would most certainly be a good decision," Alix said to her sister before fixing her gaze on Anne. "Why have you joined us? I don't believe you came down here simply to chat."

"I have decided that I shall be attending the ball after all," Anne stated.

Her cousins were pleased by the news, their eyes brightening with excitement as they leaned forward in their seats.

"I'm glad to hear that," Tessa said with an energetic head nod. "Speaking only to Bernice for most of the ball would be truly intolerable."

The fiery and portly form of Bernice Eversley strutted into the room, halting the flow of conversation. "Girls! We must head out to the carriage right away—" She paused at the sight of Anne, her lips forming a thinly veiled disapproving pout. "Well? Have you come to bid us goodbye?"

"On the contrary, I have come to inform you about my change of mind regarding the ball. I would like to be in attendance," Anne replied.

Her aunt's countenance changed immediately, her scowl melting away and replaced by a pleased smile.

"This is lovely news!" Bernice cried out, covering the distance to pat her approvingly on the shoulder. She rang a nearby bell, summoning two maids who appeared almost immediately. "Do you recall the blue and white gown I had made for Anne? The immensely fashionable one? Do bring it here at once."

Anne had to grudgingly admit that Bernice's insistence on purchasing extravagant, ball-worthy gowns had proven useful this once. Although she was certain Cedric wouldn't think less of her if she appeared in average clothes, it wouldn't hurt to look her best.

As the first maid hurried away to heed the order, the other maid listened carefully as Bernice rattled off instructions regarding pieces of jewelry that were to be brought to her as well.

"You might as well sit down while we wait," Alix said, gesturing to an armchair opposite the sofa she reclined.

"That's a good idea. I had best conserve my energy for the dance sessions bound to occur," Anne replied, claiming the seat.

Tessa stepped away from the pianoforte, joining her sister on the sofa. "I quite like the Chivonian dance style, although the circular motion occasionally causes my head to spin."

"It has the same effect on me," Alix said, agreeing. "Without a doubt, the waltz is the best dance of all."

"I am neither great nor terrible at dancing, which leaves me with little to say regarding the topic," Anne admitted.

Tessa nodded vigorously to show that she understood. "That's quite alright. Dancing is the sort of subject that reveals itself through action rather than discussion anyway."

Her uncle's familiar figure appeared in the doorway. His eyes swept around the room, his eyebrows lifting imperceptibly to find her present.

"It looks like you changed your mind about attending the ball after all," her uncle commented.

Anne shrugged. "I have come to realize that some nights are better spent in the company of others."

"It is never too late to live differently," he replied, nodding in approval. He tapped his ivory cane against the ground thoughtfully before continuing, "I daresay you shall find the music lovely tonight. Do have an enjoyable time."

"I most certainly will," Anne responded, although she doubted the music alone would be riveting enough to garner her interest.

"Good! The gown's here," Bernice exclaimed upon the maid's return. She turned to Anne and made a shooing motion, "If you get dressed now, we should arrive at the ball within the hour."

"That sounds like a lovely arrangement," Anne replied, hopeful that the ball would prove more entertaining than the others she'd attended.

Chapter Ten

Cedric arrived at the architectural behemoth of a townhouse belonging to the Palmerstons, who were good friends of his mother. That was a major reason why he'd chosen to attend the ball, the other being that Anne had requested him to. Her letter had been unexpected but well-appreciated, adding intrigue to an otherwise uneventful evening.

He joined the crowd of fellow attendees as they made their way toward the entrance and strolled in the direction of the ballroom. The air reverberated with a harmonious overture played by an orchestra in the minstrels' gallery. Walls lined with glided mirrors reflected the warm glow of crystal chandeliers and the deliberate movements of those present.

He scanned the group of people, wondering if Anne had arrived. The gathering of stylish women wearing gowns in various trendy patterns proved colorful enough, but none of the ladies were striking enough to catch his eye. A second scan of the room revealed the familiar forms of his friends, Lords Haynes, Blackwood, and Cobridge.

"Stonehaven! I wasn't aware that you had returned to London," commented Blackwood as Cedric drew nearer. Raising a spirited eyebrow, he motioned to the other men. "Given the unsurprised look on your faces, I gather this is common knowledge."

"You spend all your time traveling back and forth on various expeditions," Haynes explained with a casual shrug. "Cobridge and I have pressing duties that keep us in England and, by extension, London and its news. Regardless, that does not explain why Stonehaven has failed to call upon us since his return."

"My sincerest apologies, gentlemen. Urgent matters have demanded my attention, leaving me with little time for social calls," Cedric explained.

Cobridge grinned and patted him amicably on the shoulder. "You're already forgiven, old friend. Pay for the first round of drinks the next time we're at White's, and I'll completely wipe the matter from memory."

"That sounds like an excellent arrangement," Cedric replied, nodding his head.

He and his friends shared the same background of being the lords of esteemed houses, but that was where their similarities ended. Blackwood was a skilled swordsman, the great-grandson of an accomplished warrior, with a brimming zeal for adventure. Tales of his travels often served as conversation pieces during gatherings at White's and similar clubs.

On the other hand, Haynes was a natural negotiator, loved by friends and grudgingly respected by foes. It was largely speculated that he was heavily involved in commercial pursuits, a rumor he neither rebuffed nor confirmed, shrouding his public profile in mystery.

Cobridge was an avid art lover and frequent patron of the theater. He was often found hosting private play readings, visiting art galleries, and sponsoring opportunities that fostered artistic talents. He was also one of Cedric's oldest friends, as they had known each other since infancy.

"Speaking of urgent matters, it has come to my notice that you're courting Lord Eversley's niece," Haynes said.

Cobridge's face lit up with interest. "Lady Anne, isn't it? That's a rather lovely name."

"Is that true, Stonehaven?" Blackwood asked, turning to him. "I didn't expect you'd be struck by Cupid's arrow so soon."

"It would appear that a spell of the good variety has been cast on me," Cedric responded, infusing his voice with a softness that made his statement more convincing. "I found other ladies wanting, but Lady Anne's combination of attributes has captivated me entirely."

Cobridge laughed. "You sound completely besotted."

"What could possibly give off that impression?"

"We're only a few minutes in, and you've already begun singing her praises," Haynes said plainly. "I have never known you to be a poet."

Blackwood's mouth curved in amusement. "During the course of my travels, I have witnessed many men turn to marriage despite expressing their immunity to the parson's mousetrap."

"And what is your assessment of it?" Cedric questioned.

"I consider it a positive development," came Blackwood's quick reply. "Love is a brilliant occurrence when it's genuine."

"It is, truly," Cobridge said in agreement. "However, for all my interest in arts and fanciful poetry, I'd sooner refrain from it until a few years have passed."

"It's what any sensible young gentleman would do," Haynes explained. "Regardless of society's attempts to present it otherwise, marriage is an economic contract that must be approached sensibly."

"Regardless of differing opinions, our friend here has obviously fallen in love," Blackwood declared with a pleased smile.

"I wouldn't go as far as to state that," Cedric said, unable to keep himself from objecting. "My feelings for Lady Anne border more on admiration, given that she's an intelligent woman."

Haynes' eyebrows lifted. "You have been courting the lady so determinedly because of admiration?"

"Men have pursued women for worse reasons, such as wealth or beauty," Cedric stated.

"It certainly doesn't hurt that Lady Anne happens to have all of those traits," Blackwood responded.

Cobridge cleared his throat and yanked awkwardly at his cravat. "I happened to call on Lady Anne once during the previous season. Her disinterest in me was quite obvious, although she remained kind and polite."

Blackwood chuckled. "The question Cobridge means to ask is this: how have you managed to grab the attention of a great beauty?"

"I did so by being handsome and charming," Cedric replied with a slow head shake. "It's a shame you've let the familiarity between us keep you from seeing that."

"I wouldn't call you charming, but perhaps that is because I'm not a lady," Haynes said. "You can be unbearably blunt when the situation calls for it."

Cedric turned to him with an inquiring look. "Do you consider it a bad trait?"

"Not at all," Haynes admitted. "In actuality, I admire your straightforward approach to things."

"It's an invaluable skill, one I should do well to learn someday," Cobridge added.

"Feel free to stop by my home for a few lessons," Cedric began to say, his words trailing off as he caught sight of Anne.

Over a dozen pairs of eyes swiveled in her direction as she walked into the ballroom alongside her family. Dressed in a high-waisted gown with intermixed blue and white colors, she moved with an unpretentious grace that was both striking and endearing.

Excusing himself from the gathering of friends, he crossed the room and made his way toward Anne. Her face lit up the second she spotted him, a slow smile spreading across her face.

"I'm delighted that I didn't have to spend much time searching before spotting you," she said with relief.

Cedric chuckled. "I'm glad I could be present to assuage some of the awkwardness you're feeling. You look beautiful, my lady."

Anne averted her eyes, clearly flustered. "You aren't required to keep up pretenses whenever we meet in polite society."

"Believe me, I'm not doing this for the audience," came his abrupt reply. He scanned their surroundings for eavesdroppers before continuing. "While our arrangement may be false, not every word that leaves my mouth is the same."

For a second, he was taken aback by his own statement. Was he ... flirting? No. He was merely being complimentary, he told himself.

"That's rather nice of you," Anne said, the coloring in her face deepening. She took a steadying breath and let out a long sigh. "I don't often feel like I belong here. If I want entertainment, I'd prefer reading books in the library."

"Which is perfectly acceptable," Cedric responded. "High society likes for us to follow tradition and eschew our personal inclinations. But it's a glorious thing to be unique, with specific interests and habits that stand out from the rest."

She paused and stared at him directly, "Do you truly think so?"

"I do," he replied. "Your approach to life is different and refreshing, which is why I enjoy being around you."

"I should be the one saying that," Anne said, tucking a lock of hair behind her ears. "You're the reason why I was granted leave to work in the first place."

"Clearly, we're each valuable to the other," Cedric said as the music slowed and the first set was announced. He held his hand out and glanced at her expectantly, "Would you care to dance?"

"Only if you promise not to take offense at my average dancing skills."

Another chuckle escaped him. "I promise you, Anne. I wouldn't dream of doing such a thing."

He led her to the dance floor, where other ladies and gentlemen were already gathered. They stood close to each other, with Anne placing her hand on his upper arm while he linked her other hand with his.

They moved in time with the music as he guided her body through gentle turns and measured footwalks.

Cedric's thoughts seemed to fade into the background as his mind processed the minimal gap between their bodies. All he could think about was Anne and how nicely she fit in his arms.

"You dance well," he noted. "I believe you were being modest by saying otherwise."

"I didn't say I was terrible, just average."

"Perhaps this experience will make you inclined to attend more balls."

Anne pursed her lips thoughtfully. "I suppose so. It's rather nice to dance with a skilled partner."

Cedric held her gaze. "Is that all I'm good for?"

"Certainly not."

"Then share what features you like best about me."

Her answer came quickly. "I admire your ability to keep a cool head no matter the situation."

"Is there anything else?"

It was not lost on him that his questions had the effect of making her flustered. He enjoyed the look of shyness that typically crossed her face in such situations.

"I like the way you smile and chuckle."

Cedric blinked. "Did I hear you correctly?"

Anne nodded, growing braver. "It is just as I've said."

"Well, that doesn't sound very flattering."

"Only a man would say that about such a compliment. A woman would be pleased to hear that she has notable smiles. Would you rather have me highlight your frowns and scowls instead?"

"I'll have neither, thank you."

"More importantly, you've recently become an important element in my life, and I fear what things will become once our arrangement ends."

"It won't be the end," Cedric vowed, compelled by an unknown force to tuck a stray strand of hair behind her ear. "Even if I were at the far end of the earth, I'd come running upon receiving your letter."

He noticed she was staring at him intently, her gaze heavy with emotions he couldn't identify. Before he could ask, the music came to an end, and Anne stepped away from his hold.

"There's my cousin Alix. Most likely, she has some interesting details to share regarding the ball."

Cedric nodded. "Very well. Thank you for accepting my invitation to dance," he offered his arm, satisfied by the familiar pressure of her arm on his. "Let me escort you to join your cousin."

"No," Anne replied, shaking her head for emphasis. "My apologies, but I'd like to do so alone."

Cedric watched as she left the dance floor, moving briskly in the direction of Lady Alix. Although the dance was over, his nerves buzzed with the knowledge that the experience he just had was unlike any other.

***

Anne had changed out of her clothes and was sitting quietly in the Eversley garden, surrounded by fireflies. The peaceful environment couldn't be any more different from the turbulent thoughts in her mind. Why had she felt so astounded during the duration of her dance with Cedric? It was a pleasant sort of feeling but an unfamiliar one nonetheless.

It was unlike anything she had ever experienced. His words, gentle gaze, the way his hand rested against her back ... she had replayed the moment over and over in her mind since the ball ended an hour ago.

It was a good thing she joined Alix as soon as the dance finished—otherwise, she might have blurted out something inappropriate or entirely embarrassing. Cedric was a gentleman with whom she was having a fake relationship, Anne reminded herself. Whatever she was feeling had to be gotten rid of.

Where did it come from anyway? She and Cedric presently shared a mutually beneficial arrangement, one she'd been perfectly comfortable with upholding. He was kind and supportive, the perfect choice of individual to have in one's corner.

Since their first meeting, she had considered him a valuable companion with interesting attributes. But after the ball, Anne felt as though her life would be incomplete if he wasn't around permanently.

The sound of approaching footsteps alerted her to someone entering the garden. Although it was nighttime, the lamp light made it possible for Anne to see. Felicity's boots made a slight noise as she marched along the gravelly path before she settled on the wooden bench next to her.

"It's late, I know," Felicity said, taking off her bright pink hat. "Will you chance a guess as to why I'm here?"

"I'm doubtful any reason I provide will be accurate."

"Colin and I have just returned from paying a visit to his grandmother," came the reply. "We stopped by because I wanted to ask you how the ball went."

Unsurprised by yet another example of her cousin's quirky tendencies, Anne accepted the explanation. "You're in luck because there's a lot to say. Where's Colin?"

"He's somewhere in the house, conversing with my father," Felicity replied. "Now you've piqued my interest further: what happened at the ball?"

"The event went well," Anne said, suddenly hesitant to say more. "There were no scandals, fortunately, and the music was skillfully played."

Felicity rolled her eyes. "You know well enough that replies of that kind aren't enough to satisfy my curiosity."

"Lately, I have begun to feel a sudden attraction to Cedric," Anne blurted out. "It seems as though it's come from nowhere."

Felicity blinked. "That's not surprising. He is, after all, a handsome man."

Anne frowned. "I'm afraid you don't understand. My work is my priority, and I never went out of my way to seek his attention."

"Most likely, your feelings for him were there all along, and you've only just realized it."

"Is that even possible?" Anne muttered. "I consider myself a self-aware individual."

"I may not be a love expert, but I know a little bit about feelings," Felicity's eyes went momentarily to her wedding ring. "Such instances can occur."

Anne's eyebrows furrowed further. "It's just so hard to believe."

"I may not know much about Lord Stonehaven, but the little I've learned tells me he's a good individual. He knows more about you than the average suitor and is accepting of it all: your ambition, intelligence, and so on," Felicity paused to smile softly. "He reminds me of Colin, who supports me in all endeavors."

"Even if I were to consider an actual relationship, Cedric isn't ready to settle down."

"What if he's changed his mind?"

Anne sighed as she massaged her temple. "He hasn't. He's only participating in the fake courtship because he believes there are no romantic feelings involved. Were I to suggest otherwise, he'd likely shut such an attempt down adamantly."

"What if he doesn't?" Felicity pressed.

Anne stifled a yawn and rose from her seat. "Even then, there's a chance things would remain awkward, and I'd rather not have that."

"It's too late to head home, so Colin and I will stay over for the night," Felicity said, also standing up. "I hope you'll make the best decision."

"I already have," Anne responded without further elaboration.

Chapter Eleven

Cedric strolled along the smooth hallway to check out books in the library. It was a grand room, spacious and designed with a large, airy window. Rows of polished shelves were stacked along the walls, occupied by books of varying sizes and subjects.

Sunlight filtered in, providing more warmth to an already cozy environment. Since waking up that morning, he had been unable to stop thinking about a book that caught his eye earlier. Titled *A Chronicle of Events: Unveiling Mysteries of the Distant Past* and written by a fellow named J. Hawthorne, Cedric was certain it was full of immense historical knowledge.

There were other books by the same author, but this one was said to be rare, having had its publication discontinued upon the author's death. After several minutes of searching, Cedric found the book in the back row and picked it up.

Although he had only minimal interest in *A Chronicle of Events*, he knew it was precisely the sort of book Anne enjoyed reading. He glanced out the window thoughtfully, debating whether to pay a visit and give it to her.

Would she appreciate the gesture or be upset that he'd interrupted her free time? Cedric hoped for the latter. He doubted he could wait until work resumed before seeing Anne again.

"I had hoped to find you here," Jasper murmured, cradling his head as if in pain as he entered the room.

"What's the matter?" Cedric asked, although he already knew the answer.

"I have a headache from drinking too much the previous night."

Cedric shot him a disapproving look. "For someone who handles alcohol badly, you do too much drinking. Did you visit the gambling halls?"

Jasper nodded, his mouth twisting distastefully. "Yes, I did. I also lost all my money in the process."

"Why would you make such a decision?" Cedric asked, unable to keep the frustration from his tone. "Surely, you knew it was unlikely to amount to anything positive."

"I thought I might be able to double the sum, but I was wrong," Jasper said, frowning. "The men at the table were more skilled at betting than I was."

"I wish you wouldn't keep making such terrible choices."

"And I wish you wouldn't be so judgmental," Jasper retorted. "Not all of us are inclined to have the same average interests."

"You could be spending your time on more valuable activities."

"Gambling counts as that for me."

Cedric shook his head in disappointment. "All it does is make you lose money."

Jasper folded his arms. "That's because I'm not playing the game correctly. With more practice, things will take a turn, and I shall emerge a winner."

"You're better off tossing all your money in the gutter."

"I've had it with you talking down to me," Jasper said, scoffing loudly.

"I'm merely offering needed advice," Cedric stated.

Jasper turned to him with a mocking glance. "How ironic, coming from you of all individuals."

"What do you mean by that?"

"Just because your horses win races doesn't mean you aren't considered as lowly as I am. Many people consider you extravagant for transforming a good piece of land into a horse breeding center."

Cedric's jaw clenched. "It's a prosperous center which has made the family immense profits with minimal losses."

"You can keep saying that to convince yourself," Jasper said, his face twisted in a sneer. "You and I are the same. We practically have no glorious aspirations, just two spoiled young men wasting their years and doing nothing remotely useful."

The book firmly secured in his grasp, Cedric made toward the door. "I'm not like you."

"Truly? Because to me, we may as well be twins."

"You couldn't be more wrong," Cedric said as he left the library.

He didn't stop walking until he was out of the house and in his coach. As the vehicle rolled out the gates and sped along the road, he attempted to think over what just happened.

Jasper's antagonism had been unprecedented, and worse, he seemed to believe every statement he uttered. Cedric had no reason to consider himself similar to his cousin. For one, he wasn't the sort to indulge in wasteful habits, nor was he proud of participating in such acts.

No, he was different from Jasper, he told himself. He had transformed his interest in his horses into a profitable endeavor. He was an upstanding member of society, one who bore his family name without stain or atrocious behavior. Still, Jasper's words rang repeatedly in his mind, hurting him deeply.

The coach drew to a stop outside the Eversley household, and the footmen called out greetings as he stepped out. Cedric decided he'd hand the book to the butler and visit the family at another time.

As he approached the door, he noticed a tall woman with prominent smile lines standing on the threshold.

"Good morning," Cedric greeted. He observed that the woman bore some resemblance to Anne, although he doubted he'd ever seen her prior.

"Good morning, Lord Stonehaven," she replied with a friendly smile. "My name is Felicity, and I'm Anne's cousin. Are you here to visit her?"

"I was hoping to hand this book to the butler so he could deliver it to Anne."

"Forgive me, my lord, but I must insist on you coming in," Lady Felicity responded, already walking into the house. "A few minutes of your time is all I require. I want to know all about my cousin's new suitor."

"A brief discussion sounds reasonable," Cedric replied, unable to refuse the invitation. He followed Lady Felicity into the drawing room, where another gentleman sat poring over a newspaper.

"Colin, have you met Lord Stonehaven?" Lady Felicity announced, drawing the man's attention. "Lord Stonehaven, meet my husband, Lord Sheffield."

Lord Sheffield rose to his feet, bowing slightly. "Delighted to meet you, Lord Stonehaven."

"The pleasure's mine, Lord Sheffield," Cedric replied with a brief bow.

Cedric surveyed the man, appreciating the seamless tailoring of his clothes and his reliable demeanor. He could see why Lord Sheffield and Lady Felicity were a couple; she was the flame, diverting more light to his reserved disposition.

"How often do you find yourself thinking of Anne?" Lady Felicity asked, a playful smile on her lips.

Her husband groaned, palming his face. "Fels, you can't just ask that!"

"Lord Stonehaven has granted me permission to ask any questions I desire," she glanced at him for confirmation. "Isn't that the case?"

"It is," Cedric responded, amused by her straightforwardness. "The answer to that is often. I think about Anne often."

Lady Felicity nodded satisfactorily. "That's precisely what I expected you to say," she said, retrieving a bundle of handwritten notes. "Are you a lover of games?"

"Occasionally," he replied. "It depends on what the game is."

"Next, I'd like to ask you several questions about Anne. The goal is for you to answer correctly," she explained.

"I'm ready to begin."

"Good," Lady Felicity said, her eyes glinting with mischievousness. "What's Anne's favorite meal?"

"This should be entertaining," Lord Sheffield muttered, leaning forward with interest.

"Anne doesn't have a favorite meal," Cedric responded. She had mentioned that to him during a lunch break at work, explaining that she preferred a variety of different flavors instead.

"Correct!" Lady Felicity exclaimed, looking pleased. "Now, onto the next question."

Cedric smiled, further warming up to the prospect of an exciting game. In addition, he found Lady Felicity and Lord Sheffield very likable. "I eagerly await the challenge."

***

Anne descended the stairs, moving in the direction of the drawing room. The news that Cedric had come to visit was both unexpected and joy-inducing. Why had he dropped by to see her? she wondered, hastening her steps.

Her mind was already made up regarding her unresolved feelings for him. She had decided to wait a few more days to see if she felt differently before taking any steps. In the meantime, she was determined to enjoy each day and bask in every happy moment.

Upon entering the room, she saw Cedric, Felicity, and Colin reclining comfortably in their seats. As usual, Cedric was impeccably dressed in a dark waistcoat paired with a gray tailcoat, his mass of curly hair properly styled. The sight of him was enough to make her stumble, but she maintained her stride and gave no hint of her emotions.

He looked especially pleased as he murmured something, and Felicity cried out, 'Correct!"

"I see you all have decided to play a game without me," Anne said, taking a seat.

Cedric grinned. "My apologies, but if you had joined us, there would be a clear winner."

"Why is that the case?"

"We were quizzing Lord Stonehaven on how well he knows you," Felicity explained.

"And how has he done thus far?"

"He got four questions out of five correctly. That's pretty impressive," Colin responded.

Cedric flashed her a smile. "Spending long hours in each other's company tends to have that effect."

"Not necessarily," Anne replied, returning his smile. "It also depends on how well the other person pays attention."

"I stopped by to give you this," he said, handing her a book.

Her eyes widened as she examined the item. "A rare J. Hawthorne publication. I've searched far and wide for this," she murmured, flipping the pages in wonder. "My parents owned one once, but they lent it to someone who ended up misplacing it."

"I'm glad you like it. It would certainly serve more purpose in your library than mine."

"Thank you for the kind gesture," she replied, smiling warmly.

Felicity coughed gently, drawing their attention. "I'd like to part ways with two tickets to an exclusive museum opening happening in a couple of hours. Colin and I have plans to watch a play instead, which is why I'm giving them out."

"An exclusive museum?" Anne asked. "What differentiates it from an average museum visit?"

Felicity shrugged. "Exclusive museums cater only to elites and learned individuals. There will be personal guides, and tons of knowledge lay waiting to be gained."

"That does sound like a splendid experience," Anne replied, warming up to the idea. The prospect of being surrounded by historical relics and fossils was too good to pass up.

"I'll take the tickets," Cedric told Felicity before turning to Anne. "Would you be interested in attending the opening together?"

"I'd love to."

Cedric grinned. "While you get ready, I'll see if I can answer more of your cousin's questions."

"Prepare yourself. The questions are about to get tougher," Felicity warned.

"I have the feeling he'll ace it regardless," Anne said proudly, rising to her feet. "I'll change into a day dress and return shortly."

She left the room in a hurry, eager to return to her bedchamber and prepare for an eventful day. Her feelings for Cedric seemed not to have waned. Instead, his mere presence was akin to a bright lamp showering everything in light.

It felt nice to see him getting along with Felicity. The fact that he won a game based on how well he knew her was also flattering.

As soon as she returned to her bedchamber, a maid aided her in changing into a blue gown with a crescent design along its waistline. Anne picked out a hat as an accessory to her outfit. She liked to wear them occasionally, although she preferred her hair uncovered and loosely tied.

When she returned to the drawing room, Cedric was lounging on a couch with no signs of Felicity and Colin in sight.

"They have left for the theater," he explained. His eyes scanned her figure for a second before he continued. "You look lovely in that gown."

"I appreciate your kind words. Do you like visiting the museum?"

He nodded. "When I was a young boy, my mother brought me along on her numerous trips to museums."

"My parents did too. I particularly enjoyed peering at the antique items."

Cedric stood up and tucked her hand into the crook of his arms. "Then we must waste no time in leaving so you can experience that again."

"I shall be back by evening," she informed Barnaby before her exit. She allowed herself to be helped by Cedric into the waiting coach, the wind tugging at her bonnet as the vehicle sped down the road.

"I admire the strong bond shared between members of your family," Cedric shared.

"It's an Eversley trait," Anne replied, tilting her head proudly. "We're on good terms with everyone, even distant cousins thrice removed. Is your family the same way?"

"We love one another dearly, although our attitude toward wholesome daily interactions is admittedly cavalier."

"You have a brother and a sister," Anne recited, tucking a hand under her chin. "I'm an only child, so I can't say I understand what that's like."

Cedric raised an amused eyebrow. "Clearly, you've been doing your fair bit of research."

"I was curious," Anne admitted, blushing slightly. "But that's as much as I know."

"I urge you not to feel embarrassed. I find the effort flattering."

"That's a relief. Would you be willing to share a bit about your family?"

He nodded. "Rhys and I are close, likely because there's only a two-year difference between our ages. Daphne is growing into a lovely woman, and I enjoy her company, although her interests these days lie in a successful entry into society."

Anne made a sympathetic sound. "I don't blame her. Such procedures can be daunting."

"Was yours the same way?"

She giggled as her mind raked over memories from the past. "I was too occupied by my books to notice. I breezed through the events in mute haste, expending little energy until it was time to return home."

"Let me guess, your reticence was mistaken for shyness."

A mischievous smile played on her lips. "Correct. It wasn't a horrible entry, as far as debuts go."

"Daphne will make a smooth transition as a debutante. My mother will make sure of that," he remarked.

"She sounds like a strong-willed woman."

"You don't know the half of it," Cedric replied, shaking his head. "The woman can move mountains if the situation calls for it."

"But you love her all the same."

"I do. I find her tenacity annoying at times, but it's a quality that's occasionally admirable."

"And your father?"

"He enjoys living in the country and training his dogs. I plan to pay him a visit soon enough."

Anne adjusted the sleeves of her gown. "That's quite lovely. My cousins are like the siblings I never had. Alix and Tessa have enjoyable witty quips and jokes, whereas Felicity and myself are similarly aged and the best of friends."

"I enjoyed Lady Felicity's convivial nature," Cedric said.

"I'm glad you did. She's special to me, and I'm relieved you two get along well."

"It appears we've arrived," Cedric announced as the coach clattered to a halt in front of a grand museum. He went out first before extending a hand to help Anne alight.

She did so gracefully, the expensive fabric of her gown allowing for easy movement. She took a minute to admire the lofty building before they ascended the steps and entered the museum.

Inside, the atmosphere buzzed with the low murmurs and footsteps of visitors. The high windows let rays of sunlight in, illuminating a variety of antiques—glass displays, carved figurines, and ancient weaponry with striking designs.

Anne paused in front of a marble statue of a Roman general. "It looks almost human. Undoubtedly, art is a reliable conduit for translating the physicality of the formerly living."

"I agree that it helps us understand historical figures better," Cedric replied.

She moved on to a white wall lined with paintings from ancient Greece. "A lot of these were made by amateur painters, many of whom were poor apprentices with minimal sponsorship."

"The intriguing part is," Cedric added. "If someone had told them their pieces would be hanging from the walls of a museum centuries later, they would never have believed it."

Anne nodded, pondering his words. "They were merely inspired individuals pursuing their dreams."

"There's a lesson here if we're willing to see it."

"Which is?"

"Not all pursuits are worthwhile. Take the case of the Greek artists: their apprenticeship did nothing to seal their legacies. On the other hand, their devotion to art yielded more value."

"We have made equally useful decisions," Anne replied. "Me, with my interest in history, and you, with your affinity for horses."

"Being a stud farmer is decidedly less impressive when compared to your intellectual penchant."

"That isn't true. You have accomplished a fair amount in that field of interest."

Cedric's face grew solemn. "I have merely been playing a child's game. It's high time I turned to more meaningful activities."

"Do you truly believe that?"

He turned away stiffly. "My endeavors as a stud farmer serve no one except rich wealthy men who wish to entertain themselves."

Anne stepped in front of him, taken aback by his negative statements. "I don't believe any of that to be true."

A resigned look crossed his face. "Even if you don't, the fact remains that my time could be put toward better avenues."

"Did you know horses in the past had feeble strength and were incapable of extensive travel? It was through careful breeding that humans managed to make them stronger and more efficient. That's thanks to stud farmers like yourself."

"You're right," Cedric replied. "And in horse racing, the best horses go on to create better breeds."

"Precisely," Anne said. "You're more valuable than you realize. Your occupation is far too complex to be referred to as child's play."

A smile tugged at Cedric's lips. "I'll do well to remember that. Thank you, Anne."

"You're welcome," she replied, glad to have gotten her thoughts across. "I do not consider your interests any less important than mine."

"I'm relieved to hear that," he responded, exhaling deeply. "My cousin, Jasper, considers my horse breeding venture a waste of time. He informed me of that during a recent argument."

"He's wrong, and I'm willing to debate that at any moment," Anne emphasized with certainty. "It's the most ridiculous statement I've ever heard!"

Cedric chuckled, drawing closer and offering his arm. "Henceforth, I'll take less advice from him and more from you. Now let us resume our exploration of this museum."

Anne wasted no time in taking his hand, letting him lead her further down the room. As they made toward a large portrait, a man dressed in a scruffy tailcoat and breeches too stained for polite company approached them.

"Lady Anne! Is that you?" He exclaimed, lips parting to reveal rows of rotting teeth.

Never one to discriminate based on appearances, Anne enquired politely, "May I help you with something?"

"My name is Lawry, and I work as a secretary at The Society of Antiquaries of London," Lawry revealed, still smiling. "I heard about your work at the dig, and I must say it's an incredible accomplishment. Are you truly certain the artifacts are original?"

"Completely certain," Anne replied with a nod. "I tested for age, the quality of the material,s and craftsmanship to achieve the results. Also, I'm glad to meet with a member of the society."

"Brilliant," Lawry praised, rubbing his palms together. It was an unnerving gesture for reasons she could not exactly place. "I wonder how much the artifacts would cost if they were on sale."

"The pieces will most likely not be on sale," Anne said firmly.

"It was only a joke," Lawry responded, tilting his hat in a departing gesture. "It was lovely to meet you, my lady. I must now take my leave."

"That was an unusual conversation," Cedric observed as they watched Lawry leave the building. "His presence grew increasingly hard to tolerate by the minute."

It probably wasn't surprising that the Society of Antiquaries of London had members with less refined personalities than expected in polite company. Men like Lawry often disregarded life's ordinary pleasures for perceived higher pursuits, all the while thinking themselves better than others. Anne couldn't help but be glad that her interactions with them thus far were severely limited.

"He's likely the sort of intellectual who takes pleasure in unsolicited questions," Anne replied, placing her hand on his arm. "Let us continue. Hopefully, there will be no more distractions."

Chapter Twelve

A cloud of dust rose alongside Cedric's carriage as it sped down the long path leading to the fruit of his investments: Stonehaven Stud. As always, he felt a jolt of pride each time he glimpsed the imposing gates of his stud farm. Where there had been nothing once, now stood a booming establishment responsible for raising healthy stallions.

Bright red roofs gleamed under the afternoon sun, and a plethora of sounds lingered in the air—the constant whinnying of nosy horses, the determined footsteps of grooms as they discharged their duties, and the clanging of horseshoes.

His carriage pulled to a stop, and Cedric emerged, his tall figure descending without difficulty. He was still reeling from the excitement of the previous day when he'd spent an entertaining evening in Anne's company.

The visit to the museum resulted in a closer bond between himself and Anne. It had also given a needed closure to the conflict with Jasper.

Anne's reminder that his stud farm was just as important as any other endeavor affected Cedric deeply.

It renewed his belief in his strengths and bolstered his confidence. Never again would he let Jasper's words shake him so deeply, Cedric mused.

It was a shame he couldn't bring Anne along on his visit. He doubted her uncle would grant her permission to venture north of London with a man who wasn't kin.

In any case, he and Anne were expected to resume work at the archaeological dig the next day. He could hardly wait for the hours to roll by until he could see her again. He missed spending time around her, flipping through the pages of a book while she studied antiques.

The head groom, a stocky man named Harold with kind eyes set in an angular face, approached with a respectful bow.

"Good afternoon, my lord," Harold greeted. "Would you like a report on the foals?"

"Most definitely," Cedric replied.

The two men proceeded along the expanse of land as Harold provided a detailed narration of the births and upbringing of the newborn foals. Cedric listened patiently, his eyes glinting in pleasure as they entered the stables. A long examination of the animals showed that they were well-fed and thoroughly taken care of.

The foals nudged his hand affectionately as he patted them.

"Have you named them yet?" Cedric asked, spotting an Arabian thoroughbred foal with a bright white coat and an adventurous glint in its eye.

"Some have names, although that's changeable if you so wish," Thomas replied.

"That one," Cedric said, pointing to the Arabian. "Does he have a name yet?"

"Not yet."

Drawing nearer, Cedric watched as the animal trotted spiritedly around the paddock, full of endless energy. "We'll call this one Racer. I have the feeling he'll win a number of medals soon enough."

After receiving essential updates regarding the state of the stud farm, Cedric and Thomas discussed upcoming races and new training schemes. He was satisfied by the smooth operation of the establishment, certain that it was on its way to becoming the best in London.

An hour later, Cedric returned to his coach, fulfilled by the joy of time well spent. Jasper was wrong—Stonehaven Stud was a worthy investment, incomparable to an insignificant night spent gambling away all of one's money.

Smiling to himself, he leaned back in his seat as his coach sped along the road. When his vehicle slowed in a residential area, Cedric glimpsed a familiar figure strolling along the pavement.

"Morton?" He called out in a questioning tone as his coach slowed to a stop.

His friend spun around, his eyes growing friendly with acknowledgment.

"Stonehaven, I heard you were back in London. It's nice to have that confirmation for myself."

"I'm more curious as to why you're strolling leisurely along the rugged streets of London."

Morton shrugged. "I recently took up cricket, and I'm certain I can hold my own against ruffians. I also decided against bringing my carriage in order to maintain a low-profile identity. Would you like to join me in attending a cricket game?"

It was just like Morton to be found in unexpected places. Cedric considered the question before nodding slowly. It wouldn't hurt to take on another hobby, especially one that improved his physical abilities. "Depends. Where's the venue?"

Morton grinned. "We're already there," He pointed to an imposing iron gate some yards away. "I must warn you, cricket is a physically demanding sport."

"I already knew that," Cedric replied, stepping out of his coach.

"Feel free to dismiss your driver," Morton said. "I have a special hackney that picks me up after every training session."

Cedric did as suggested, and the two men slipped past the gates and ventured further into the vast cricket grounds. It was a large space consisting of a bright green field and a pavilion on the right end for spectators.

A group of men were already standing in the field, some chatting while others practiced their swings. A man in a distinctive gray outfit stood at the center of the gathering, handing out praise and critique in the same breath.

"Good afternoon, Daufner," Morton said pleasantly, approaching the man.

"I have a new swinging style for you to practice today, Morton. A natural like yourself should have no difficulty learning it," Daufner responded in a deep, gruff voice. "Who's your friend?"

"This is Stonehaven. He's new to the cricketing world."

Daufner nodded. "Nice to meet you, Stonehaven. Are you willing to devote your time to mastering the art of cricketing?"

"In truth, I haven't quite made up my mind yet," Cedric replied honestly.

"That's fair," Daufner said. "You'll begin the session by pairing with Liam over there."

Liam was a muscular man with a shaved head and an imposing figure. Cedric had the feeling he was being tested. If that was the case, he might as well put on a show.

Mirroring the slightly crouched position he'd witnessed other cricket players make, Cedric gripped a bat firmly in hand. In one fluid movement, with a powerful swing, Liam sent the ball over at breakneck speed. Cedric brought his bat down to meet the ball, narrowly making contact. It wasn't spectacular by any means, but it created enough momentum to send the ball sailing in the air.

"That's enough," Daufner called, shooting Cedric a look of appraisal. "For an amateur, your form and swing looks promising. I'm confident it'll get better with more practice."

"You did great," Morton murmured as Daufner barked instructions to another pair of men.

"Thank you," Cedric responded, glad he'd spotted Morton when he did. "It appears engaging in a new hobby is a satisfying task after all."

***

Anne hurried out of the house toward Cedric's carriage as the morning sun rose high in the sky. Although the past few days had been interesting, it felt nice to resume work at the dig. She'd discovered a couple of books that would prove helpful in learning more about the antiques.

"I hope my timely arrival has met your expectations," Cedric said, his warm eyes sending a thrill through her as he stood in the doorway of the vehicle.

As usual, he was relaxed and properly dressed, giving the impression that he was unaffected by anything. The only notable difference was his handsome face, which had a few scratches along the side.

"I'm beyond pleased by your dedication to my cause," Anne praised, accepting his hand. With a carefulness she had come to expect from him, he assisted her into the coach.

Adjusting comfortably on the plush seat, Anne set her reticule down as Cedric sat on the opposite bench, and the vehicle began to move.

"I was going to come in, but I figured a repeat of the previous day might occur. That would only delay us further," Cedric explained.

"That was a wise decision. Felicity may be absent, but my uncle can be rather chatty when the mood hits him."

Cedric lifted his shoulders slightly. "I can usually abide that, except when you urgently need to get to work."

"Thank you for being considerate," Anne replied, cheeks pinkening. Unable to resist her curiosity any longer, she blurted out, "What happened to your face? You look as though you waded through a rough patch of thorns."

He grinned as he lifted a hand to his cheek. "Your words made me realize I was holding myself back. My mother never showed any interest in my horse breeding ventures. Neither did Jasper, except for when he wanted something in return. That caused me to become doubtful of my interests. I also refrained from trying out other hobbies."

Anne listened patiently, flattered that he was choosing to bare his heart to her.

Cedric's gaze turned serious as he continued, "It's all thanks to you, truly. I realized my interests were equally valuable as any other. Now, I have taken up cricketing, and it has been a pleasant experience."

"I'm glad that you're happy, and I hope there'll be fewer cuts as your training progresses," she replied warmly, meaning every word.

They continued to converse as the coach arrived at the dig. It was lovely to see working men scattered around the venue, immersed in their work and carrying equipment. Anne felt a rush of anticipation as she headed in the direction of her office.

It felt like a miniature home where she could be at ease and indulge in her interests without judgment.

"Excuse me, I need to check in on Hatter. I'll be right back," Cedric said.

"That's alright," Anne replied. "I'll resume analyzing the antiques in the meantime."

With Cedric gone, she entered her office and walked toward her desk. Everything looked just the way she'd left it, the box of antiques, her tools ... except for her notes. They had clearly been tampered with, given that some papers were nowhere in sight.

Anne concluded that the cleaner probably got rid of the notes by accident. Luckily, she had the foresight to make copies of the notes, and therefore her research could continue.

Anne sat behind her desk just as the sound of knocking came from the door.

"Who's there?"

"I'm a footman from the Earl of the Stonehaven's household, and I've come to deliver your lunch," a gruff voice replied.

It was too early in the day for lunch. Anne wondered if this was due to an administrative error on the part of the Stonehaven cook. Regardless, she couldn't turn the food away after the valet had come all the way to give it to her.

"Come in," she responded.

A thin man with a sparse beard entered and placed a food basket on the desk. When he took his leave, she peered curiously at the variety of food ranging from roasted trout to cream puffs. One of the biscuits looked particularly appealing, so she decided to have a taste of it.

Anne was reaching for a biscuit when the door opened, and Cedric said loudly, "What are you doing?"

"One of your footmen dropped off an early lunch."

"My household runs in a timely manner, and there are hardly any inconsistencies. My mother makes sure of that," he replied, eyebrows knitted together.

Before Anne could respond, he picked up the lemonade drink that accompanied the food and poured it over a plant in the hallway. Her jaw fell open as the plant curled into itself, dying immediately.

"Such a reaction can only be due to poison," Cedric declared with his jaw clenched. "Someone is trying to kill you."

Anne's eyes widened in shock. "W-what? I never given anyone cause to—"

"I'm taking you home immediately," He continued as he took her hand and led her out of the office. His fingers squeezed hers in one firm, soothing gesture. It was the only thing she could register through the haze of fear of shock. That, and his words. "And I'll do anything in my power to keep you safe."

Chapter Thirteen

Cedric stood with his arms folded as he watched the dig's men present themselves for investigation. He had done the right thing by taking Anne home before returning to the dig. Having her out of his sight allowed him to think rationally and properly consider the terrible situation.

Someone had tried to poison Anne. Merely recalling that fact sent an unpleasant quiver through him. Who would have cause to do something so horrible? As far as he knew, the men at the dig viewed her with great respect and showed no revulsion at being co-workers.

For Anne's sake, he'd been pleased by the encouraging environment. Now, he couldn't help but wonder if he'd been naive, preventing him from seeing things as they were. It was increasingly clear that whoever was behind this had some connection to the dig. That person knew of Anne's lunch break, as well as the fact that his household was in charge of presenting their meals.

They also knew to meet Anne when it was certain that Cedric was not by her side. If he had been late by merely one second ... Cedric paused, shaking his head to keep the terrible thought out of his head. There was no way he could let Anne return to the dig until it was certain that the harm had been averted.

That was why he'd enlisted the help of Haynes, who had strong connections with the constabulary. His friend had heeded the request without delay, appearing at the dig with two constables at his side.

For the past two hours, Haynes and the constables had questioned the workers in turns. Cedric had observed the interactions with a mix of impatience and a sliver of optimism, hopeful they would uncover valuable information.

All he needed was one good lead, be it the name of the man who falsely delivered Anne's lunch or news about a suspicious figure. Yet, there was none so far, which only succeeded in provoking him further.

Cedric tapped his foot impatiently on the ground as Haynes approached him.

"We are yet to learn anything tangible," Haynes said, his tone dripping with regret.

"None of the workers come across as ingenuine," Cedric replied, running a hand through his hair.

Haynes nodded. "There are no signs of suspicious activity on their part."

"All hope is not yet lost," Cedric gritted out through clenched teeth. "I hired a private investigator to look into the matter."

"That's a brilliant decision," his friend replied, nodding in approval. "You're holding up well, given the pressure."

Cedric headed in the direction of the exit, Haynes trailing closely behind. "I stopped by the investigator's office after escorting Anne home safely. I wanted to make sure all possible options were covered."

"Excellent. We could use the extra help."

Cedric stepped past the gates and saw the investigator he hired, a balding man with a solemn countenance. He was accompanied by two burly men who stood on either side of a rangy man with closely cropped hair, effectively trapping him in place.

"Mr. Felton. Are there any updates?" Cedric asked the investigator.

"My men and I traced the carriage that delivered the food," Mr. Felton explained, gesturing for the rangy man to be brought closer. "We found the coachman, but he claims he has little knowledge of what happened."

Cedric acknowledged the words with a brief nod before turning his attention to the coachman. "It would be best for you to start talking."

"I didn't mean to poison anyone," the coachman said pleadingly. "Earlier this morning, a strange man paid me to deliver food to this destination. I only did as requested."

Cedric released a disappointed sigh, knowing the coachman was telling the truth. "Did you see what he looked like?"

"N-not really," the coachman stammered out, his eyes wide in fear. "It was the crack of dawn, and I could barely make out his face."

"How tall was he?

A reflective look crossed the other man's face before replying, "S-slightly taller than me."

"Did he have any distinctive attributes?"

"I-I don't think so."

Haynes readjusted his hat and turned away. "I don't believe we'll learn anything new from this individual."

"I agree," Mr. Felton said with a nod of his head. "We'll take our leave now. I'll be sure to inform you when I uncover something new."

"I don't think I've ever been more disappointed in my life," Cedric said to Haynes, massaging his temple.

Haynes laid a supportive hand on his shoulder. "You're highly stressed and anxious. You need to go home and rest."

"And leave the investigation unattended to?"

Haynes raised an eyebrow. "I'm more than capable of overseeing matters here. You, on the other hand, are far too high-strung to be of help."

"I'm not going anywhere," Cedric interjected. "I'd feel better knowing that we're one step closer to finding the man who attacked Anne."

"Let me remind you again. You'll be of no help to anyone until you've had a proper sit-down," Haynes replied firmly. "If you truly care for Anne, then going home is the right thing to do."

Through the haze of his anger and frustration, Cedric saw the logic in his friend's statement. With Haynes and the constables investigating the dig, as well as Mr Felton and his men prowling the streets for information, there was little he could do in a highly emotional state. He was far too rattled by the realization that Anne had nearly been poisoned to process any other thoughts.

"Very well. I shall take my leave," Cedric responded. "Send word as soon as there's any information."

"I assure you, I shall," Haynes promised.

Trusting in his friend's words, Cedric boarded his coach, a burning sensation playing in the pit of his stomach. For a while, the dig had seemed like a safe environment where Anne could pursue her dreams and conduct research.

Given what happened, would she ever feel comfortable to resume work again?

It upset him deeply to think that someone out there had tried to sabotage her efforts. Anne would not be wrong to prioritize her safety, but he hoped the encounter would not keep her from engaging in her interests. She was a brilliant woman who deserved to live as fully and loudly as anyone else.

On his part, all he could do was protect her. He refused to stand aside and let her be harmed or cowered into nonaction.

The slowing of the coach's wheels signaled that he had arrived at his family's townhouse. Cedric hurried out and acknowledged his butler's greeting with a brief nod before making his way down the hall.

His mother, sister, and brother were gathered in the drawing room, playing a board game. Their attention turned to him as he entered.

"You look as though you've seen a ghost," Rhys pointed out with a concerned look.

"He's right," Daphne said. "You look pale and more stressed than I have ever seen."

His mother rose from her seat and hurried forward to caress his face. "My dear, did you encounter something terrible?"

Cedric nodded, not bothering to hide his agitated state. "Someone attempted to poison Lady Anne, the woman I've been courting."

His mother gasped, raising gloved hands over her mouth. "That's incredibly cruel! Who would ever do such a thing?"

Cedric's frown deepened. "I'm hoping to find out soon."

"You should sit down," Rhys suggested kindly. "Shall I hire a private investigator?"

Cedric sank into one of the plush settees, a sigh escaping him. "I have already done so. I can only hope we find the culprit before time runs out."

Daphne dabbed at the corner of her eyes with a handkerchief. "I cannot imagine how terrified Lady Anne must be feeling. Is she home at the moment?"

He nodded. "At present, she is being tended to by her family."

"We must send calling cards to the Eversleys at once," his mother said in a determined voice. "The poor girl needs all the support she can get. Daphne and I will pay her a visit tomorrow."

"That won't be necessary," Cedric replied with obvious hesitation.

He had refrained from sharing the full details of what occurred for the sake of Anne's privacy. However, there was a chance his family would learn more than they needed to by visiting the Eversleys.

"For the past couple of weeks, you've been courting a woman whom you've never bothered to introduce us to," his mother said, her hurt visible in those stormy gray eyes he also shared. "Paying her a visit in these trying times is all I ask."

"Please, Cedric. We would be terrible people if we didn't go see her." Daphne urged.

Rhys nodded in agreement. "That sort of kind gesture isn't bound to hurt anyone."

Cedric sat rigidly, resisting the urge to blurt out that it was a fake courtship and there was no true obligation for his family to visit the Eversleys.

He made a gesture of approval. "Very well. I am certain Anne and her family will appreciate your visit."

***

Felicity hurried down the hallway toward Anne's bedroom. As she entered, she glimpsed her cousin's slender figure sitting up in bed. Although she was dressed comfortably in a woolen gown, dark rings had appeared around her eyes, signaling stress and a lack of adequate rest.

Felicity went to her bedside, pulling her in for a hug. "My darling Anne, I rushed over as soon as I could. Are you alright? Don't you worry; we'll find a way to resolve this."

Anne closed her eyes, sinking further into the hug. "I am trying not to dwell on it."

Felicity drew back momentarily, scanning her cousin's body. Luckily, there were no scars or injuries. It was clear the damage to Anne was more psychological than physical. There was a paleness to her, one that could only have resulted from a traumatic experience.

"I-I am so sorry, Anne," Felicity continued, a sudden wave of emotion rushing through her. "I cannot imagine how terrified you must have felt."

"It was shocking, to say the least," Anne replied, resting against her bed's wooden headboard. "I didn't expect that my place of work would become so deadly."

"It's a dig, for goodness' sake. It's the last place anyone would expect to be poisoned," Felicity said. "Shall I call a physician? Have you eaten? Would you like to rest some more?"

"You don't have to fuss over me. I'm alright. How did you hear about it?"

"News spread quickly about a young lady who was nearly poisoned at a dig, so I hurried here to confirm," Felicity answered. "Luckily, no one else seems to know it's you."

Anne nodded, her relief showing. "It's a good thing I refrained from talking about my entire identity."

"That's a smart decision. Otherwise, the ton would gossip relentlessly about it."

"I suppose I'm not at risk of being ruined today."

"Thankfully so," Felicity replied. "There are much better days ahead to potentially ruin your reputation."

That elicited a tiny smile from Anne. "Small mercies. Cedric was kind enough to bring me home immediately, and for that, I'm grateful."

"I wonder what Lord Stonehaven is up to."

"He seemed quite upset before he departed," Anne responded. "He promised to find the culprit and bring them to book."

Felicity smiled in approval. "That's precisely what I expected of him."

Her cousin's eyes softened. "Whatever he's currently doing, I just hope he's fine."

Such a statement only served to confirm Felicity's hunch that Anne loved Cedric but wasn't aware of it. "You should rest, Anne. You've had quite a stressful day."

"I have to agree," her uncle said as he entered the room. Frown lines had appeared on his face, providing an image of sadness and relief. "You mustn't let that awful experience stand in the way of a good rest."

"Thank you for your concern, Uncle," Anne murmured, already beginning to doze off.

"You're welcome," he softly replied. He and Felicity stepped out into the hallway, careful to shut the door quietly behind them.

"You mustn't blame yourself for this," Felicity told him. "No one could have foreseen this."

"I am the one who granted her permission to work at the dig."

"Only because you wanted her to find happiness."

"It's partly my fault."

"Not at all," Felicity said. "The only one to blame is the individual who attacked Anne."

Her father managed a smile, patting her head in an affectionate gesture. "Thank you for the reassurance, Felicity. I'll be in my study if you need me."

Having confirmed that Anne was unharmed, Felicity headed downstairs, where her assistant waited patiently in the entrance hall.

"How is she?" Johanna asked.

"She's a little shaken up, but otherwise, she's fine," Felicity replied, her tone turning resolute. "I have decided to grow more serious about getting Anne and Lord Stonehaven together."

"I can't say I'm surprised," Johanna said, a knowing smile playing on her lips. "Your persistence remains unmatched."

"Actually, I'm no longer acting out of sheer desire," Felicity responded, a serious look crossing her face. "I'm looking out for Anne."

"In what way?"

"Someone tried to poison Anne," Felicity emphasized, her eyes growing steely. "Being married to a titled, influential man like Lord Stonehaven would grant her more protection."

Chapter Fourteen

"Good evening, Barnaby," Cedric greeted as the Eversley butler let him into the house. He had intended to follow Haynes' advice and rest but found that he couldn't do so without confirming that Anne was faring well.

"Good evening, my lord," Barnaby responded. "I regret to inform you that Lady Anne is presently asleep."

"Is Lord Rutherford open to visitors?"

Barnaby nodded. "He asked me to direct you to his study when you stop by. Shall we?"

Cedric assented, and the two men made their way further into the house, where a distinctively gray door stood. As Barnaby announced his arrival and Lord Rutherford's firm voice bid him to enter, he felt a certain calmness wash over him.

The visit was not only to see Anne. He had to discuss ways to keep her safe with another man who cared for her deeply: her uncle.

"I haven't thanked you properly for bringing Anne home safely," Lord Rutherford said, pushing the documents on his table to the side.

"It was the only reasonable thing to do," Cedric replied, settling down in a chair. "I'm more preoccupied with keeping her away from future instances of danger."

"Do you have any ideas that might help?"

"I have a few," Cedric answered, "but all include curbing Anne's freedom to some extent."

"Would it interfere with her ability to work at the dig?"

"Certainly not. I would never attempt to stand in the way of Anne's happiness."

Lord Rutherford nodded, satisfied by his answer. "In that case, I'd be willing to hear your suggestions."

"We might start by stationing one or two men to escort Anne at all times, regardless of where she intends to go."

"And you?"

"I'll continue to accompany her to the dig. The men would be an additional safety measure."

Lord Rutherford steepled his fingers. "Do you think Anne will approve of this idea?"

"Not at first. I expect that she'll be adamant about not drawing additional attention to herself," Cedric responded. "In due time, she'll come to understand the logic behind the decision."

"And if she doesn't?"

"She will," he replied with certainty. "Anne is everything but irrational."

A smile played on Lord Rutherford's face. "You seem to believe strongly in her."

"I do," Cedric said without hesitation. "However, I don't expect that she'll accept this action without opposing it. She'll argue fiercely, that's for certain."

"It is clear you have more patience for her than I ever will," Lord Rutherford said with a chuckle. "I have a couple of footmen who would be glad to take on the security role."

"Excellent. I have made arrangements for the culprit to be found."

"Through a private investigator or the constables?"

"Both," Cedric replied. "I am determined not to leave any stones untouched."

"You have acted impeccably," Lord Rutherford praised. "Anne could not have a better person by her side during this strenuous encounter."

"It's too early to celebrate, not until we find that terrible man who attempted to poison Anne," Cedric responded. "I'd like to ask if you know of anyone who might have a motive to hurt her."

Lord Rutherford considered the question at length. "Anne is not the sort of woman to collect enemies. To my knowledge, she gets along with most people and prioritizes her books over frivolous hobbies."

Cedric had come to a similar conclusion himself. "It is only reasonable to assume that the person aiming to hurt her is a stranger. Might his motive have to do with the dig?"

"Most certainly," Lord Rutherford said. "There seem to be underlying politics we aren't aware of."

"In that case, I'll make it my priority to find out," Cedric replied in a resolute tone.

Just as he made the statement, a maid arrived bearing a message that Anne was awake and ready to receive visitors.

"I must take my leave," Cedric said, rising to his feet. He was thoroughly excited to see Anne again.

"I shall come with you," Lord Rutherford said, joining him. "I have yet to check on my niece properly."

The two men walked up the staircase and down the hallway, where a waiting maid ushered them into Anne's bedroom.

Anne was sitting up in bed, and a healthy pinkness had slipped into her face, offsetting the former paleness. Her lips curled to reveal a bright smile as Cedric walked in, adding more allure to her already beautiful features.

"Anne," he murmured in a voice filled with relief and concern.

"I am glad you're here," she responded as he drew closer and tucked strands of hair behind her ear.

"I'm happy to see that you're faring well. Is there anything you'd like? Water? Some food?"

She shook her head. "None at the moment."

"Are you certain?" Her uncle asked. "I can arrange for the kitchen staff to prepare a quick meal."

"That won't be necessary," Anne replied.

"I'll find the person behind the attempted poisoning, I promise," Cedric blurted out. He hoped the words would offer her needed reassurance.

Her smile grew an inch wider. "I trust that you will."

Lord Rutherford crossed the room to pat Anne's head before clearing his throat. "I must take my leave now. There's an urgent letter I need to write before the day ends. I'll send your lady's maid up to keep you both company."

He leveled a warning look at Cedric before departing the room.

"I don't think I have ever seen anything like it. My uncle puts a great deal of trust in you," Anne observed.

Cedric tilted his head. "Why do you think that's the case?"

One of her shoulders lifted. "He seems to think you're above compromising me, given that he doesn't obsess about a chaperone when we're together."

"He did say he'd be sending your maid up shortly."

"That's quite permissive compared to most guardians."

Cedric flashed her a grin. "Or maybe it's because I'm an honorable gentleman, and your uncle knows it." His face grew more serious as he continued hesitantly, "Given what occurred, perhaps you might consider working from home ..."

"I prefer to visit the dig physically," Anne objected. "It's the perfect working environment with few distractions and plenty of resources."

"I suspected you'd say that," he replied with a knowing smile. "I just want you to remain safe."

Anne turned to him with certainty. "Given the zeal with which you are pursuing this, we'll likely find the perpetrator soon."

His gray eyes remained fixated on her as he drew closer. "I'll do everything in my power to protect you."

"You have done so much for me, whereas I've barely given anything in return."

Cedric grazed the side of her face with his finger. "Don't say that. Your spirited personality is enough to repay everything twice over."

Almost as though some force beyond him was compelling him, Cedric lowered his head until his face was directly opposite Anne's. It allowed him a clearer view of the features he'd come to enjoy over the recent days. Those blue eyes as bright as the morning sky, rosy cheeks that brought to mind a blooming garden, and curved lips that enhanced their owner's expressions.

He waited a second for something, an objection from Anne perhaps, but heavy silence permeated the air around them.

Cedric pressed his lips against hers in a gentle kiss that uplifted his soul. The few seconds of it felt glorious, and as they drew apart, nothing else seemed like it would compare.

The stunned look on Anne's face brought him harshly to reality. The guilt growing within him was too much, too intense to spend another minute in her company.

He managed to utter a quick apology before exiting the room. It was only when he was back downstairs and away from her that he began to breathe again.

He was shocked at himself for initiating the kiss. Why had he behaved in such an unusual manner? It was as though all the unspoken emotions he'd experienced since meeting her finally exploded into one singular action.

The only reasonable conclusion was that he had feelings for her, which he'd failed to realize until that moment. And if that was the case, did Anne feel the same way? She had tilted her face up to seal the kiss, but did that mean anything?

Chapter Fifteen

Reclining on a chaise longue in her bedroom, Anne flipped idly through the pages of a book. Her attention was elsewhere, stuck on the events of the past hour. She felt a mix of joy and embarrassment, each emotion jostling for a prominent position within her.

Her heart had thumped continuously since Cedric kissed her, signaling that it was a wonderful experience. And yet, she couldn't help replaying how he'd reacted after. She couldn't tell if that was a positive reaction or not.

Anne sighed deeply, setting the book down. It was clear that she was deeply affected by the kiss. She couldn't keep from wondering what to do about her emotions. She liked Cedric in a manner that was more than friendly that much was certain.

She worried that a core part of their agreement was being broken by her romantic feelings for him. After all, they had agreed to a secretly platonic relationship that would serve their respective goals. News of her feelings would probably earn Cedric's annoyance if he ever came to know about it.

But why had he kissed her in the first place? Anne thought, pursing her lips reflectively. If he didn't fancy her romantically, then why bother acting in a manner that spoke otherwise?

It was likely because his emotions were jumbled due to her near poisoning. That may have caused him to mistake simple affection for a dear friend for something more. The way he stiffened and departed briskly seemed to support that notion.

The sound of knocking broke into her thoughts. Anne granted permission to come in, so her uncle and cousin strolled into the room.

"You look like you've rested adequately," the Viscount said with an appraising glance.

"Indeed, I have."

"Excellent," Felicity said, clapping her hands in delight. "I prefer seeing you up and happy than miserable. You deserve everything good, Anne."

"Thank you for saying that and for providing support."

"It's what family does," Felicity responded with a dismissive wave of her hand. "Really, we'll always be there for one other."

"Felicity's right," Uncle George added. He settled in one of the seats before continuing, "There's an urgent matter I'd like to discuss with you."

"I already know what it is, and I'm not inclined to discuss it."

"Will you listen, at least? Even for a minute?"

Anne pursed her lips before replying, "Very well."

"Will you continue to remain safe at the dig?"

"I will."

Uncle George cast her a disbelieving look. "Do you truly believe that, or is this an attempt to be defiant?"

Anne sighed. "My work is very important to me, and I've come too far to stop now."

"Surely your safety takes precedence over other aspirations."

"Ideally, I'd like both to be safe and free to pursue my interests."

"And what if you can't have both?" Her uncle pressed. "No one in their right mind would return to the same environment where they were nearly murdered."

"I'm willing to," Anne replied stubbornly. Although she understood her uncle's concerns, she refused to be cowered out of her duties at the dig.

Uncle George's eyes shone with annoyance. "Sometimes I wonder if I've made a mistake by giving you so much freedom."

"Compared to other gentlemen around, you're a sensible man, dear father," Felicity cut in cheerfully, stepping in between the two arguing figures. "And we love you all the more for it. Don't we?"

Anne nodded. "We absolutely do. I shudder at the thought of being raised by anyone else."

Felicity extended a hand. "Come. Let's go downstairs so you can get some fresh air."

Anne didn't need to be told twice. She already felt cooped up being in bed all day, so she left the room eagerly with Felicity at her side.

"Lord Stonehaven!" Felicity exclaimed as they arrived at the drawing room. "I didn't realize you were here."

"I came to see Anne and discuss matters of her safety with her uncle," Cedric replied, nodding politely as he reclined in his seat. Anne noticed that he was avoiding eye contact, looking everywhere but in her direction.

"My safety?" Anne asked, glancing at him and Uncle George for more information.

"He didn't put me up to dissuading you from working if that's what you're wondering," her uncle responded with a pointed look.

Anne blushed, relieved to hear of Cedric's noninvolvement in her uncle's earlier suggestion.

"There are other ways to keep you safe without halting your progress at work," Cedric reassured her.

"Anne's safety would be more guaranteed if she were engaged to Lord Stonehaven," Felicity ventured, turning to Cedric. "If you were to offer for her, I'm certain ill-intentioned individuals would think twice before harming her."

"The title of Earl of Stonehaven is a powerful one," Uncle George said, nodding as he considered the idea. "Few people would be willing to cross such an esteemed family."

Anne paled, shooting an accusatory glance at a triumphantly smiling Felicity. It was incredibly annoying that her cousin would make such a proposition without informing her first. She was unamused by Felicity's obvious intent to push them together despite knowing the actual context of their relationship.

"Let us take our leave, Father, and leave these two to discuss the subject," Felicity suggested, taking Uncle George's arm. She flashed Anne one last smile before they left the room.

***

A loud sigh escaped Anne as her cousin and uncle departed, steering the room into silence. Gusts of clean air drifted in through the window, accompanied by the lovely scents of flowers in the garden. Anne was aware of Cedric's eyes on her as she walked to a chair and sat, intertwining her fingers to ease the internal nervousness.

"I apologize for Felicity's behavior," Anne said, lifting her head to meet his gaze. "I didn't expect that she'd make such a suggestion."

A few seconds went by before Cedric responded. "She isn't wrong. You'll be much safer as my wife."

Anne shook her head, replying with a hint of sarcasm. "Surely, there are other options."

"There are, although this one is equally valid," Cedric replied calmly. "More so because I have compromised you."

Anne felt some degree of panic rising within her. If her inkling was correct, then he was about to say something entirely unexpected. "C-compromise?" She said in a forcibly bright tone. "There's no reason to call it that. It was a lapse in judgment."

"A lapse," Cedric repeated, his tone insistent. "You may choose to call it that, but it was behavior unacceptable of a gentleman. I apologize for kissing you, Anne. I have compromised you therefore I need to take our courtship more seriously."

"I'd rather not be married out of pity," Anne retorted.

It was enough that he didn't feel anything special from the kiss they shared. Proposing a genuine courtship only because he was riddled with guilt was even more insulting.

"I acted inappropriately, and—"

"This is a thoroughly awful decision," Anne continued with an exasperated sigh. "You have other plans for your life, do you not? To enjoy your youth fully and only marry when you're ready?"

"I did once," Cedric answered.

"Then you mustn't give up on those plans for my sake," Anne said with a note of finality. "A kiss is only considered compromising if other parties were to learn about it."

Cedric's eyebrows furrowed. "Anne, there's more ..."

"I'm more worried that the man who tried to murder me is yet to be found," she commented, changing the topic. "How's the search going?"

"I enlisted the help of two individuals in finding him. One is a close friend whom I trust wholeheartedly, and the other is a renowned detective."

"That's quite a competent team."

"So far, we've questioned the workers at the dig to no avail. Upon interviewing the individual who delivered your lunch, we learned that he was paid to do so by an unknown man."

"I have no inkling of who that person could possibly be," Anne responded genuinely. Her life consisted of historical learning, leaving little room for making enemies.

"I know you don't," Cedric replied, his tone comforting. "There's no need to worry about that anyway. I'll make sure the man is found and punished for his actions. How do you feel?"

"In truth, I'm scared but trying my best not to be intimidated."

Cedric's mouth curved in amusement. "Only you would take a murder attempt as a chance to intimidate."

Before Anne could respond, Barnaby strolled into the room with an item in hand.

"There's a letter for you, my lady," he informed her with a polite bow.

Anne took the letter, her curiosity increasing when she recognized the stamp belonging to the Society of Antiquaries of London. News of the attack must have spread quickly, prompting the society to be in contact.

"What does it say?" Cedric asked in a curious tone.

A smile appeared on Anne's face as she finished reading the letter. "Mr. Sheridan wrote to confirm my safety and express his dismay regarding what happened. He says the Society of Antiquaries of London will investigate the matter."

"That's a relief," Cedric replied. "It's nice to know you have their support."

"I must write a reply at once, assuring him that I'm alright."

"That's an excellent idea," Cedric responded, rising to his feet. "I shall hereby take my leave."

Anne nodded slowly. It was odd, but she hated the idea of him leaving. "Thank you for everything, Cedric."

"I'll always be there whenever you need me, Anne. I mean it."

He cared for her; that much was obvious. But not enough to court her genuinely without the pressure of doing so out of duty. Ignoring the pang of hurt within her, she waved goodbye as he took his leave.

Chapter Sixteen

In his tastefully decorated drawing room, Cedric reflected on his conversation with Anne. He had acted like a gentleman by making an offer to court her properly. It was the only logical way of redeeming himself after kissing her. And yet, she'd rejected that offer entirely. When she asked him if he had other plans for his life, his answer had been genuine.

He always wanted to marry later in life. That was the reason he'd enlisted Anne's aid in the first place. But in that moment, as he considered her question, he realized that the idea of marrying Anne didn't sound terrible. In fact, it brought a degree of excitement that lingered strongly in his thoughts.

If she hadn't interrupted him, he'd been willing to go ahead and express his change of mind. Although Anne's reasoning was sound, Cedric wished she wouldn't be so flippant about his suggestion. She wasn't the sort of woman to be married to out of obligation or duty. She possessed a series of qualities that could hardly be found anywhere else.

Her sound mind and sense of humor were enough to keep a gentleman occupied for the rest of his life, paired with a beautiful face that formed vivid expressions and spoke with a firm cadence.

He was not foolish enough to believe that the courtship conversation hadn't led to a strained relationship between him and Anne. She believed he had no other reason to propose a genuine courtship except duty. It was up to him to smooth things over and reassure her the alternative was the case.

He ... liked her. Deeply. So much that it felt like his heart and hers were intertwined and inseparable in every circumstance.

Jasper walked into the room with a distinct flush on his face from drinking. "I had a splendid time at the bar this evening."

"Wonderful, cousin," Cedric murmured. "I cannot claim to have had an equally pleasant day."

"Why is that the case?" Jasper asked in a flippant tone.

Cedric released a deep sigh and sank deeper into his seat. "Someone tried to poison Anne. She had to evacuate the dig, and we're yet to find the culprit."

"Oh?"

A flash of irritation crossed Cedric's face. "Indeed. Both Anne and I have had our days disrupted. Our desire is for the matter to be resolved and for things to continue as before."

Jasper scratched the side of his face. "Perhaps so."

Cedric's eyebrows furrowed. "You might want to pretend to care, at least."

"Why wouldn't I?"

"Because your countenance is one of everything but concern."

Jasper shrugged. "It isn't my fault that I'm not moved to tears by what happened to you."

"I wasn't asking you to be," Cedric replied with a dismissive wave of his hand. "I can see that I'm better off pondering the situation on my own."

Jasper shifted on his feet and scratched his head. "I'd be happy to leave and leave you to your thoughts. However, I have a favor to ask."

"What is it?"

"I apologize for the harsh words I uttered the previous day," he continued quickly. "Now, on to a more important subject. I would like for you to lend me some money."

"No."

"What do you mean?" Jasper asked, a hard edge entering his voice.

"It's just as I've said. I shall not lend you any money," Cedric replied calmly. "I'm tired of contributing to your gambling exploits, and I will not be a part of it any longer."

"You can't do this to me!" Jasper snapped, his face reddening. "I am your cousin. I am family."

"My decision has already been made," Cedric responded.

"You've just made a terrible choice," Jasper retorted before storming out of the room.

Cedric remained in his seat, too preoccupied by his thoughts to bother about his cousin's antics. He had yet to decide on the next course of action when it came to Anne. There was also the fact that the person who tried to harm her was still unapprehended. He was still thinking about this when his mother walked into the room.

"You look worn out," she noted, fixing him a worried look. "Would you like to discuss the problem?"

Cedric lifted his head. "I suppose that would help. It's a subject I haven't been able to decipher on my own."

"Talking definitely helps."

"That is a sentiment I'm inclined to agree with," he replied, running a hand through his hair.

"Well?" His mother asked impatiently. "You've kept the suspense long enough."

"That was not on purpose, I assure you," Cedric replied, sitting up straighter. "I was simply gathering my thoughts."

"I encourage you to take your time," his mother said, her eyes softening.

"I have reached a rather conflicting point in my life. If I don't resolve it, it stands to affect my bond with Anne."

His mother frowned. "In what way?"

"I am beginning to feel strongly about her, so much so that it pervades my entire being."

"Do you truly not know what this means?" She asked with a raised eyebrow.

"I am thoroughly confused by your question," he responded.

Lady Lavinia shook her head slightly and sighed. "When you think of Anne, what feelings rise to the surface?"

"I want to protect her from any possible harm. I want to be by her side at all times, appreciating the sound of her life. I want to hear all about her historical readings and other interests. I cannot conceive a better world than one with all of these in it."

His mother listened patiently with a joyful twinkle in her eyes. "This reminds me of old times."

"How so?"

"Your father was the same way, confused and hesitant about his emotions. I knew I loved him deeply, but it didn't seem like he would ever reciprocate," his mother narrated with a nostalgic smile. "When I became engaged to another gentleman, the realization that he would be losing me forever snapped him to his senses, and he came running to me."

Cedric tilted his head in puzzlement. "Is there a hidden message to this? I'm afraid I'm too high-strung to think properly."

His mother smiled broadly before continuing, "The strange feeling you've been referring to is love. You're in love with Anne."

Cedric paused to digest the information before replying slowly, "Are you absolutely certain?"

His mother nodded. "You know you're in love when a person occupies your mind and rouses your protective instincts."

It made perfect sense. His feelings for Anne had not been predictable by any means, but their strong presence could not be denied. It was why he'd found himself disregarding his other plans, replacing them with ones where she was included.

He wanted a future in which he and Anne were married, living in a cozy house with their children. Although he wasn't at all certain she felt the same way, Cedric decided courting her like a proper gentleman was a great place to start.

"I didn't think you had such a brilliant penchant for good advice," Cedric told his mother with a pleased smile.

"I'm not always demanding and judgmental," she pouted. "I can be rather helpful when the situation calls for it."

***

Anne sat at her bedside table, poring over the pages of an archaeological book. It provided estimated values of items discovered at the dig. She was surprised to find that the items if sold, would rake in a higher figure than expected. She was driven to research the knowledge out of curiosity. Ideally, she hoped that the antiques would be placed in a museum rather than being sold out.

She closed the book with an extended exhale. It was difficult to keep from thinking about her last conversation with Cedric. It was still remarkably insulting that he'd offered to court her only to be honorable, and she was glad to have rejected that proposal entirely.

Yet, a part of her was upset by his quick admission that he had other plans for his life. Plans that did not include her, which he'd have continued with if he hadn't chosen to be honorable.

What was worse, Anne was well aware that there was no reason to feel this way. It was unreasonable to be so offended by his behavior. After all, the situation was the same for her, she told herself.

She had dreams and aspirations to worry about as well ... except *she* would be able to pursue them even with him by her side.

Her cousin's friendly voice bounced along the walls as she walked in. "I was hoping you were awake. It appears I owe you several explanations."

Anne's eyes narrowed at Felicity. "That you do."

"You may not have liked my suggestion encouraging you and Lord Stonehaven to marry, but surely you see it would be a smart decision."

"It isn't the only smart decision," Anne countered. "I was taken aback because I never imagined you'd suggest that publicly."

Felicity sat next to her, placing a reassuring hand on her shoulder. "I apologize for acting rashly without seeking your permission foremost. I only wished to make a suggestion that would benefit you."

"I know," Anne murmured. "That's why I have managed to keep from being truly offended."

"I'm pleased to hear that," Felicity replied with a smile.

"Cedric is a splendid gentleman; I have no doubts regarding that," she clarified. "I hope he finds happiness in the future henceforth."

Felicity tapped the side of the table. "Is that truly how you feel?"

"I do not wish to be married to him," Anne lied, turning away. "I doubt such a union would truly work anyway. We're much better off as friends."

Felicity shot her a look full of disbelief. "Regardless of your opinion on the success of a marriage between you two, I wish to hear what you truly think of him. Have you no feelings at all?"

Anne hesitated before replying, "I like him more than any other gentleman. He understands me and makes no attempts to change me."

Felicity reached into her reticule and produced a familiar-looking item. "Here's your pocketbook. You left it when visiting my home recently."

Anne extended her hand to receive it, just as her cousin flipped to a page and pointed at it.

"Here's a list you made shortly ago regarding your preferences in a man," Felicity continued.

Anne took the book, recalling how she'd made the list on her uncle's prompting. "Why does this matter?"

"Look through the list and compare each attribute to Lord Stonehaven," Felicity said, straightening her shoulders.

Eyebrows still narrowed in puzzlement, Anne did as her cousin suggested. "Someone who accepts and tolerates my hobbies. Cedric does that," she murmured. "Honorable ... he's that as well. Considerate—he's in tune with my emotions and tries to make me happy."

She continued this way, stating each trait and a follow-up of how Cedric matched it until she arrived at the end of the list. It dawned on her that she loved Cedric deeply, more so than she had initially assumed. He was the perfect match for her in personality and ideals.

"I see you're finally realizing what has been obvious to me the entire time," Felicity pointed out with a satisfied grin.

"I am," Anne admitted softly.

She had indeed realized how profoundly she felt regarding Cedric. But would he be willing to have her in his life without resenting her in the future for derailing his plans?

Chapter Seventeen

The morning sun glinted through the windows as Anne descended the stairs of her family's townhouse. She had a bright smile on her face, brought on by the knowledge that Cedric had come calling.

Her butler bowed in greeting as she passed by him. "Good morning, Lady Anne. He's waiting in the drawing room."

"Thank you for informing me, Barnaby," she replied with an acknowledging nod before walking down the hallway. Her heart leaped pleasantly in her chest as she entered the drawing room and saw Cedric waiting patiently. He was holding a bouquet of pink and yellow flowers, and his wide grin revealed his pleasure at her arrival.

"I couldn't wait till afternoon to visit," Cedric began with an apologetic nod. "I hope that isn't an issue."

"I wouldn't have it any other way," she replied. "I practically leaped down the staircase at the thought of seeing you again."

A look of relief crossed Cedric's face. "I'm glad to hear that." He brought the flowers forward, their sweet scents lingering in the air. "I brought these for you."

"Thank you!" Anne exclaimed, completely appreciative of the gesture. "I'll have a maid place it in a vase."

She had never considered herself to be the type of woman to be impressed by flowers, but the sight of them made her heart flutter. She averted her eyes slightly, aware that his entire focus was on her.

"I'm pleased to know that this has made you happy."

"Most actions you've made have brought me joy compared to others."

He raised a playful eyebrow. "Even the proposal I made the other day?"

"That's an exception," she replied, wrinkling her nose. "I hope you understand why it made me so upset."

"I do, and I apologize for uttering that in the first place. You deserve to be courted and wedded to someone who loves you entirely."

Anne flushed a bright pink. "Those may be the kindest words you've ever said to me."

"Truly? Then I'd best remedy that." Cedric murmured, drawing closer. "A woman like you deserves to have praises sung about her."

"Is this an attempt at flattery?"

"Not at all," he responded, warmth occupying his voice. "Everything I've said is the truth."

The genuineness in his delivery stirred a warm sensation within Anne. Her cheeks still flaming, she turned away, putting some distance between them. That allowed her to regain some of her composure. Was it her imagination, or could it be that Cedric was flirting with her? There was no true way of telling, and she was better off not jumping to conclusions.

"Being at home like this during the day is admittedly unnerving," she shared, changing the topic.

"That must be a harsh adjustment to make."

"It is, although I'm grateful for the love and support I'm surrounded by."

"I know how important your work is to you," Cedric murmured.

"I'm glad you do," Anne replied. "I've decided to stay away from the dig for a few more days. That's all I can manage before resuming my assessment of the artifacts."

He nodded. "That time frame should be more than enough to find the culprit. What do you plan to do now that you're home?"

"Life will be the same as before I gained employment, I suppose," she responded. "I hope to brush up on my knowledge of native tribes."

"That's a great idea."

"And you? Other than conducting investigations, what will you be doing with all that free time?"

"Visiting you, I hope."

"Every day?"

He turned to her with a raised eyebrow. "Do you object to that?"

Anne shook her head, unable to keep a smile from spreading across her face. "I'd like that very much."

"Is that a bouquet of primroses?" Her aunt exclaimed, entering the room with her uncle in tow. "I didn't know they were in season already."

"They are," Cedric responded. "It's nice to know they're well-appreciated in this household."

"My wife here loves her flowers," Uncle George shared, his words accompanied by an affectionate pat on Cedric's shoulder. "There's a tip if you ever have cause to seek her approval."

"I'll keep that detail in mind," Cedric replied.

"He doesn't need to seek my approval. He already has it," Bernice replied, setting the flowers delicately on a table. "Consider me irrevocably impressed."

"In that case, we ought to invite him to dinner, don't you think?" Uncle George asked his wife. "I believe it's past due."

"That's a lovely idea," Bernice said, looking pleased and turning to Cedric with an expectant look. "It would be an honor to have you join us for dinner tonight, Lord Stonehaven."

"Call me Cedric or Stonehaven if that's preferable," Cedric said. "And the answer to that is yes. A lovely evening spent in the company of Anne and her family sounds ideal."

Her uncle and aunt nodded in approval before departing from the drawing room. Anne tucked a strand of hair behind her ears, ever aware of the powerful presence of the man standing beside her.

"For a fake courtship situation, we've done rather well. My family loves you."

Cedric's gray eyes pierced deeply within her with his gaze. "I hope they continue to because I plan to make this relationship a real one."

"What did you say?" She asked, blinking in disbelief. It was hard to determine if she'd heard him correctly or if her mind had somehow conjured the words.

"It is as you've heard. I want to make this real, Anne. I no longer want this to be a fake courtship."

"Is this still about the kiss and redeeming yourself?"

"Not at all," he responded, holding her gaze. "I care for you, Anne, more than I have cared for any other woman. I no longer wish to delude myself into thinking a simple friendship would be satisfactory. I'm looking toward something long-term, a permanent union."

As she listened to him speak, Anne was certain she was the happiest woman in the world. A wide smile spread across her face, and she drew closer to him.

"Finally. I thought you'd never say that."

Cedric took her hand and kissed it. "I apologize for keeping you waiting."

"That's alright. We have plenty of time henceforth to make up for it."

Dropping her hand gently, he fixed her an apologetic look. "I'm afraid I must leave now. I have another meeting with the detective."

"Enjoy the rest of your day."

"I most certainly will, given the new development between us," Cedric replied, flashing her a pleased grin. "I'll see you at dinner."

Anne watched as he departed, still heady with joy from the interaction they'd just had. She and Cedric fit like a glove, perfectly tailored to a lady's precise measurements. He was the only individual who made her feel entirely fulfilled.

***

Cedric was let into the Eversley townhouse just as the dinner bell rang. He had grown accustomed to visiting the household, and from the looks of it, so did the staff. The butler received him with a friendly smile, which was eagerly returned.

As he made his way to the drawing room, it occurred to him that he'd visited the Eversleys more regularly than any other family in a long while. Each time, he'd been made to feel welcome and never out of place. He was looking forward to dining with Anne's family, fully certain it would be a pleasant affair.

He had never imagined he would grow accustomed to a set of people like this. For a while, he'd enjoyed exploring the world individually and being preoccupied with his unique endeavors. Now, that was no longer the case. He was no longer a sole entity, with only himself to think about and prioritize.

Thoughts of Anne and her preferences now occupied his mind. He liked knowing that she was well and would give anything to bring more smiles to her face. He enjoyed being around her family precisely because they loved her as much as he did.

His eyebrows lifted slightly as he noticed a new addition to the drawing room: two sets of circular mirrors hanging from the walls. His mother had purchased the same items some months before. It appeared they were the ton's new fashion objects of choice.

"I was beginning to think you'd never arrive," Anne said, appearing in the doorway. Cedric's breath caught at the sight of her in a lavender satin dress and hair piled high in a neat bun.

"Why is that? Am I late?" He asked with some alarm, thinking he might have misheard the bell.

Anne shook her head, a bright smile playing on her lips. "Not at all. Our earlier conversation still feels slightly unreal. I have yet to fully process that you care for me, and we're now courting."

Cedric flashed her a smile. "I hope my presence here has confirmed that for you."

"Most definitely," she replied.

His eyes raked over her beautiful face, committing the curve of her cheekbones and other exquisite features to memory. He enjoyed the person he was around her, someone who felt incredibly motivated and optimistic about good outcomes in the world.

"I'm pleased that you seem happy," he divulged, unable to sever the meaningful gaze they shared.

Anne raised an eyebrow. "Why wouldn't I be?"

"I know how badly you wished to resume employment at the dig. I can only hope you may return soon."

"That would be a cause for joy," she admitted, drawing nearer. "However, I'm happier because you're here with me."

"Forever and always," Cedric promised. "I'll only ever depart from your side if you insist on it."

"I'm afraid that'll never happen," Anne responded. "We're in this together for the long haul. You've made me a better woman, one who feels better equipped to navigate the world."

"Love birds!" Tessa called, hovering in the doorway with an amused glint in her eyes. "We all await your presence in the dining room. Don't worry, I shall refrain from telling anyone about the sappy statement I just overheard."

Cedric chuckled. "That's a promise I don't feel compelled to hold you to. For anyone to learn about the love I bear for Anne is a wonderful thing."

Anne blushed, her ears turning an adorable shade of pink. "You have such a splendid way with words."

"Would you be willing to join my family for dinner tomorrow night?"

"I'd love to. Your family is highly esteemed in society, but my excitement is entirely due to your remarkable self."

Cedric beamed at her compliment as he led her in the direction of the dining room. Anne's family was already gathered around the dining table, their welcoming comments filling the air as he took his seat.

Lord Rutherford looked satisfied, a soft glow present on his face. Anne's cousins, Tessa and Alix, could not contain their eagerness as they thanked him for accepting the dinner invitation. Lady Rutherford made a point of extending more invitations and praising his compatibility with Anne.

Dinner was soon served, and everyone occupied themselves with their meals. Cedric enjoyed the savory taste of the boiled cod, making a mental note to ask his kitchen staff to adopt the same cooking technique.

"We ought to begin planning for the wedding," Lady Rutherford announced, setting her spoon down.

"Surely, that's a bit too forward," Alix responded dryly. "The man hasn't even proposed yet."

"That is of minimal importance," Lady Rutherford retorted. "It's typically advised to begin planning months ahead."

"By whom?" Tessa questioned.

"The wedding column of the newspaper, of course! I understand the reluctance to begin early, but it's a most wise decision."

"There are more urgent matters to prioritize at the moment," Anne said.

"I'm quite aware of that," Lady Rutherford replied. "As far as I know, no rules prevent one from pondering several issues at the same time."

"As long as it isn't too burdensome for you," Anne replied with a slight lift of her shoulders.

Lady Rutherford blinked, clearly surprised by the easy concession, before nodding satisfactorily, "Not at all. I enjoy planning such events, and we'll be better for it."

"There are no doubts about that," Lord Rutherford said, nodding in agreement. "You're a prodigy in event planning, and your aid would be well appreciated."

Cedric observed the wholesome exchange, noticing how respectfully conflicts were being handled. Anne and her aunt were no longer argumentative, each making compromises whenever possible.

"Speaking of things one is good at, your stud farm seems like an amazing place to visit," Alix complimented him.

"Perhaps you'll take us to visit sometime?" Tessa prompted.

"Only after I've shown Anne first," he replied with a grin. "The rest of you are welcome to visit after."

"We wouldn't have it any other way," Lord Rutherford replied.

Cedric leaned back in his seat, feeling a wave of positive emotions wash over him. He was glad he'd accepted Anne's invite to dine with her family. The thrum of happy voices and the wafting scent of delicious meals gathered around him, creating a warm feeling that made his life feel complete.

Chapter Eighteen

Anne was impressed by the charming allure of the Steele household. Double mahogany doors with silver highlights gave way to a spacious entrance hall. A golden chandelier hung from the ceiling, casting its warm light upon everything. Finely brushed paintings of esteemed ancestors lined the walls, each woven with a burst of color and talent.

A woman with graying brown hair and impeccable posture joined her in the doorway. Her mouth curved politely. "My son plans to join us shortly in the dining room, so I have come to welcome you in his stead. My name is Lavinia, and I'm Cedric's mother."

"It's a pleasure to finally meet you," Anne said, a nervous flutter in her chest. Lady Lavinia's gray eyes, the same as her son's, were scrutinizing as they raked over her form.

"I could say the same," Lady Lavinia replied, interlinking her gloved fingers in a prim gesture. "Anne—may I call you Anne?"

"Most certainly."

"My son has spoken a great deal about you. It's absolutely wonderful to finally have a face to the name," she continued. a small smile appearing on her decidedly formal face.

Anne released the breath in her lungs, partly relieved that Cedric's mother didn't entirely disapprove of her but also because Cedric had spoken to his family about her. It provided a kind of reassurance regarding his feelings for her and how much he held her in high esteem.

Feeling significantly more confident about her visit, Anne nodded. "I feel the same way. Cedric holds his family in great esteem, so I'm glad to meet you all."

"I was deeply sorry to learn about the attempted attack on you. No one should ever go through such a terrible situation," Lady Lavinia said, her steely eyes growing warmer.

"Luckily, I'm not entirely scarred by what occurred."

"My daughter, Daphne, and I called on your family shortly after the incident," Cedric's mother revealed, tugging briefly at her pearl necklace.

Anne blinked in surprise. "Truly? That's such a sweet gesture. I'm afraid my family failed to mention that to me."

"It's easy to forget such details when a lot is going on."

"Your effort hasn't gone unappreciated."

As far as first impressions went, Lady Lavinia was the ideal image of a distinguished lady of the ton. She had an esteemed family name, a clean reputation, and abundant wealth that rivaled the top families in England. Her opinion was held highly, and her approval was often sought. She was used to having her way, and people flocked around her due to her position and influence.

Yet there was a softness about her that translated into kindness. In a way, it reminded Anne of Cedric and proved further that she wouldn't go wrong by becoming a part of the Steele family.

"Now that introductions are out of the way, it's high time I took you to the dining room," Lady Lavinia declared, walking down the sleek hallway until they reached a room at the right corner.

It was wide and airy, just like the rest of the house, with walls painted white and two large windows adorned by flowery curtains. A grand table sat in the middle of the room, surrounded by polished mahogany chairs.

"Is she here already?" A light feminine voice questioned earnestly from behind.

Anne turned to see a beautiful blonde woman several years younger who bore a striking resemblance to Cedric himself.

"Anne, meet my daughter, Daphne."

"It's a pleasure to meet you finally," Anne said with a polite courtesy. "Your brother has spoken so caringly about you."

"I, too, am eager to meet the lady who has brought Cedric much joy in recent days," Daphne replied with a soft smile. "You're as beautiful as I expected, Lady Anne."

"Call me Anne. I hope we'll be good friends."

"I'm certain we will be," Daphne responded, shaking her head in an affirmative gesture. "And please, call me Daphne."

"We ought to take our seats, ladies," Lady Lavinia said firmly. "Our meal will be served soon."

Anne settled in a chair, appreciating the plushness of the furniture against her body. In a way, most things here reminded her of her family's townhouse, except the designs were flashier and more refined.

Minutes later, three men joined them in the dining room. One was brown-haired, with almost black eyes and an unfriendly way about him. Anne guessed that was Jasper, the controversial cousin Cedric had once told her about. Her hunch was confirmed by the introductions, and an uncomfortable feeling raced through her when his chilly gaze met hers.

The second man was dark-haired, gray-eyed, and wore a friendly smile that put her at ease. She thought his name, Rhys, matched his easygoing nature and firm way of speaking. Although he was Cedric's younger brother, his collected manner made him seem much older.

And lastly, there was the man who made her heart race wildly. Cedric looked unfathomably handsome in his dark frock coat and matching trousers. He flashed her a smile as he covered the distance between them, settling in the chair beside her.

"Are you enjoying your visit thus far, Anne?" He asked as their meals were being served.

"I am," she replied. "Your mother was very kind and welcoming."

"That's a relief," he responded, looking pleased. "My mother can be considered overbearing by some. I believe she has a soft spot for you."

"I'm happy to hear that," Anne said genuinely. She had been worried about not being liked by his mother, but the opposite had occurred. "She is a striking woman, and I find her composure admirable."

"She is, indeed," Cedric replied, nodding in agreement. "I apologize for my delayed arrival. Rhys challenged me to a game of whist, which we played until an hour ago. I hurried to prepare for your arrival and asked my mother to welcome you instead."

"What he failed to mention to you is that he lost that game. Twice," Rhys added.

"Only because I was too busy deciphering your new strategy," Cedric retorted.

Rhys chuckled in amusement. "One of my clients is adept at whist and several board games. I was lucky to gather a few helpful tips."

"You must be a brilliant whist player now, given that," Anne noted.

"Better than the average woman, certainly," Jasper said, joining the conversation. Anne couldn't shake off the suspicion that his words were directed toward her.

"And man," Rhys corrected. "Safe to say it'll take several months before any of you can beat me at whist."

"We'll see about that," Cedric replied with a grin.

More conversation flowed easily throughout the dinner as various topics were discussed. Anne felt perfectly at home in the company of Cedric's family, with the exception of Jasper. She told herself it was only a fluke, and he'd warm up to her more as time went on.

Dinner came to a close and Lady Lavinia bade her goodbye before heading upstairs for an early sleep. Everyone else retired to the drawing room except Jasper and Cedric, because the former had insisted on Cedric accompanying him as he enjoyed a cigarette in the garden.

At first, Anne was content to watch Rhys and Daphne play a game of chess, but as time went by, she began to consider going in search of Cedric. It was high time she said her goodbyes and prepared to head home.

***

Cedric stood impatiently in the garden next to Jasper, who took a long inhale from his porcelain smoking pipe. He wasn't surprised by his cousin's insistence on being kept company as he smoked, but he wished this was occurring at a later time. With Anne around, he could hardly focus on anything else. He wanted to be around her, to speak to her, and listen to the unique cadence of her voice.

"I haven't had a proper smoke in a while," Jasper commented, exhaling a ring of miniature cloudy fumes.

"What do you mean? You do this nearly every night, so much that Mother has begun complaining," Cedric muttered.

His cousin rolled his eyes. "But today is different. You're standing next to me, which brings back memories of when we were at Eton."

Cedric faintly recalled days when Jasper suggested walks while promising not to smoke, but it would only take a few minutes before he pulled out his pipe. Now that he thought about it, his cousin's behavior then was a precursor to the present. In a way, he'd always been inconsiderate and unreliable.

He shook his head slightly before replying, "I don't smoke, and I do not enjoy being around smokers."

"Because it gives off an overbearing scent?"

"It also makes my eyes water, an unnecessary sensation."

Jasper smirked. "You're only saying that because you've barely tried it."

Cedric remained unamused. "I'm quite certain things can be disliked without being tried out."

"There's no true way to be absolutely certain unless you try."

Cedric turned to his cousin with a raised eyebrow. "Is this your way of trying to convert me into a smoker? This is only your hundredth attempt."

Jasper raised his hand in a faux innocent gesture. "It was merely a suggestion, one you're free to accept or reject."

"I'll leave you with no doubts regarding where I stand. The answer is a firm no, as it has been for many years."

They stood together in silence as the slow breeze caused the surrounding flowers to sway moderately. Jasper took another drag of his pipe before speaking.

"I had better luck getting Rhys to see things from a smoker's point of view."

Cedric's mouth twitched at the mention of his brother. "I doubt you had little to do with it. The man had been itching to get his hands on a pipe right before he left home for university."

Jasper tugged at the hem of his coat. "I remember giving him tips on how to improve his smoking experience, but it turned out he didn't need any at all."

"He was always a quick learner. He picks up interests and hobbies easily," Cedric responded, trying to keep the judgment of his tone. "And he knows when to drop the useless ones."

"Smoking is a common practice among upper-class men. It is socially acceptable, and many titled gentlemen participate in it."

"Not all of them."

"Don't be a prude," Jasper countered, his tone dripping with annoyance.

Cedric smoothened his coat and fixed him with a nonchalant look. "You asked for my opinion, and now you have it. There's no reason why we should have this conversation so regularly."

"We can agree to disagree this time," Jasper said with a wave of his hand. "The ogre and the prince have found themselves at an impasse."

"I never said you were an ogre."

"There are certain things better left unsaid. It is in prime British fashion to imply them instead."

Cedric dragged a tired hand across his face, not quite sure what his cousin was getting at. "You're not an ogre, and that's the final statement I'll make on the subject."

"Maybe I am an ogre. A greedy one at that," Jasper continued, looking off into the distance. "But as humans, we all act in ways that serve us."

"It might be best for us to talk about something else," Cedric suggested, not in the mood to decipher Jasper's cryptic statements.

His cousin's moods changed as easily as the weather and were sometimes difficult to keep track of. It was better to steer clear of the confusing ones entirely.

"Perhaps that might be best after all," Jasper conceded, taking another long drag of his pipe. He turned to Cedric suddenly, a strange look coming into his face. "Have you thought properly about the earlier plan? You promised you would inform me if there were any changes to make."

Cedric frowned, confused by the rapid change of topic. His cousin's odd look was startling, to say the least. Jasper also seemed to be talking about something he had no knowledge of.

"I don't understand what you're talking about," he replied.

Was this one of Jasper's numerous pranks? If so, this was certainly not the time for it. He was too focused on heading back indoors to see Anne again to fully entertain anything else.

"You most certainly do," Jasper said firmly. "It's too late to pretend you don't."

"I shall ask again. What are you talking about?"

"Since you've chosen to pretend as though nothing occurred, I'll take the liberty of explaining it all over again," Jasper replied, forming his words with a certain deliberateness. It was almost as though he was performing for an audience.

Cedric made a gesture for him to continue. "Very well. Go ahead."

"A few days before," Jasper began, emphasizing each word. He flicked a tiny piece of tobacco from his coat. "You and I hatched a plan that involved tricking Anne and getting the dig's historical items from her. We also made arrangements to sell them to them to the highest bidder."

Cedric's first reaction was confusion. He had done no such thing, and to suggest so was absolutely unforgivable. Anne was much too precious to him to hurt in that manner, and even if she wasn't, he wasn't the sort of individual to cheat and steal from others.

As far as jokes went, Jasper had gone too far. Before Cedric could say anything in his own defense, he heard a loud, pronounced gasp. Swiftly, he turned around to see a teary Anne standing at the garden's entrance.

Chapter Nineteen

Tears blurred her vision as she hurried away, aware of Cedric's footsteps as he chased after her. She could hardly believe her ears, the words ringing over and over in her mind. The evening had gone so well, and a final conversation with Cedric was all it needed to end on a high note.

That was why she'd gone searching for him in the first place, to express her gratitude for a day well spent. In doing so, she had stumbled upon a discussion that would likely haunt her for the rest of her life.

Would she ever heal from a betrayal as great as this one? It was highly unlikely. As she walked, her heart felt like it had fallen to the ground and shattered into tiny pieces.

To love was to open oneself to betrayal.

To love was to have one's heart sliced into and turned inside out.

Jasper hadn't said much, but the few lines uttered were all that was needed to change her worldview entirely. She had fallen head over heels for Cedric, certain that his feelings for her were genuine. They made a good match, after all. He was charming and kind and didn't feel threatened by her intelligence. He liked that she read books, spoke at length about history, and made regular references to events from the past.

She had been foolish to believe all of that. Cedric only pretended to be in love with her so he and Jasper could gain access to the dig's historical items. It only spoke to how awful he was, given that he hardly needed more money to fund his lifestyle.

Even though Anne's first instinct was to trust Cedric and deny Jasper's words, the look of guilt on Cedric's face when he spotted her was enough to dissuade her. Why else would his blood drain from his face so blatantly? Moreover, who knew him best? She, who had only known him for a couple of weeks, or his cousin, who had known him all his life?

It was all too much to think about. All Anne wanted was to return home and be far away from the awful situation that had just occurred. Perhaps with enough time, she could sort out the conflicting thoughts.

"Anne, please wait!" She heard Cedric call again before hastening her steps. She had the feeling if he truly wanted to, he'd catch up to her. Instead, he followed closely, providing enough space for her to turn around on her own.

It was the least he could do after drastically breaking her heart, but she was still grateful for it. She darted out the entrance of the grand townhouse, inwardly relieved to have brought her carriage.

"I wish to head home right away," she informed the driver before climbing into the vehicle.

"Anne, please listen to me," Cedric pleaded. "I assure you it's not what you think."

She refused to look at him, afraid of finding the truth in his eyes. More tears flowed down her cheeks as the carriage hurried past the iron gates and sped down the road.

Tonight's dinner had seemed like the perfect start to a blooming bond with Cedric's family. The meals were tastefully made, the people were friendly, and the ambiance was wonderful. She had been thrilled to meet his composed mother, sweet sister, and friendly brother, certain that her addition to the group would be a perfect fit.

Her current feelings made her earlier thoughts seem laughable. For someone who had been raised in a sheltered environment, the recent days were like being thrown into a raging ocean. Someone had tried to kill her for no visible reason other than that she was working at a dig.

While recovering from the fearful event, she had sought relief in the presence of her friends and family, as well as Cedric. Knowing he was by her side made her feel in control and complete.

Clearly, she had made herself vulnerable to someone who could not be trusted. That slow realization made her feel even more devastated.

Anne managed a relieved smile when the carriage arrived at her home. Her head hurt from crying, and there was nothing more she wanted than the privacy of her bedroom.

She walked into the house and found Tessa and Alix conversing in the hallway. Both women gasped the moment they saw her before rushing to her side with concerned looks on their faces.

"What is the matter?" Alix questioned, looking her over. "You look sad and miserable."

"Did something happen over dinner?" Tessa asked before shaking her head. "Don't answer that. Let's help you upstairs. It's clear you need some space to help properly arrange your thoughts."

"I would truly appreciate that," Anne responded.

The calming presence of her cousins proved helpful as they walked up the stairs together. It provided much-needed companionship at a time when she felt all alone.

Anne sniffled, blinking rapidly to keep more tears from rolling down her cheeks. The warmth of her bedroom felt like a welcoming hand, providing respite from an awful night.

"Shall I have a maid bring up some water?" Alix asked kindly.

Anne shook her head. "I just need some rest, thank you."

"We'll leave you to rest now," Tessa said, patting her hand comfortingly. "And remember, we're here if you require support."

Anne nodded, climbing into bed as her cousins exited the room. She would have to inform them of all that occurred the following day. Her family would be greatly disappointed to learn of Cedric's schemes, given how much affection they had come to hold for him. Her cousins, especially, would bear a longstanding grudge that would last to the end of time.

Anne sighed deeply. She wished it wasn't the way. She'd felt immense happiness for a period of time, only for it to be snatched cruelly away.

There were several other feelings to consider, but the only thing that stood out to Anne was how broken she felt.

***

Cedric watched as Anne's carriage sped off, filled with dismay. The one evening he'd hoped would turn out perfectly was everything but. He had imagined a day spent in the company of the woman he loved, enjoying the sight of her bonding with his family. He'd planned to remind her of the strong feelings in his heart, further sealing the sweet words they had already shared.

Now, life couldn't be more bleak, and Cedric could only blame himself for heeding Jasper's request to join him in the garden. At the thought of his scheming cousin, he felt a rush of rage burst through him.

Never in a lifetime would he have imagined that Jasper would sabotage him so. His cousin had gone from participating in a normal conversation to spewing absolute nonsense. It hurt to recall that now, the distraught look on Anne's face upon hearing the awful sentences. What did she think about him at that exact moment? He couldn't blame her for believing Jasper's words, given how sudden and unexpected they'd been.

Cedric returned to the garden, where Jasper idly stood with his smoking pipe. The sight of his unbothered cousin only increased his annoyance.

"Why did you do that?" He demanded.

"Do what? I was just saying a few things when she came in and hurried away," Jasper replied, his tone expressing his lack of interest in the conversation.

"Her name is Anne," Cedric said through gritted teeth. It was clear that his cousin disliked her, although the reason was yet unknown.

"Ah yes, Anne, the woman who all of a sudden has become the center of attention," Jasper said, his tone heavy with disgust.

"You're jealous of her? Is that it?" Cedric asked, taking a threatening step forward. It took everything in him not to punch his cousin precisely in the face.

Jasper turned away. "I'm only saying life was much better when you spent time with me. That doesn't mean I had a sinister motive involving her."

"I don't believe you," Cedric responded coldly, grabbing Jasper's shoulder until he faced him. "Tell me why you lied, and I might rethink the fitting punishment in my mind for you."

"What fitting punishment?" Jasper asked, his face growing pale. "You wouldn't do anything to hurt me—"

"I can and I will," Cedric cut in, a dangerous glint in his eyes. "I have far more influence in London than you ever will. I can get two cadets to lock you up where no one will ever find you."

Jasper wavered, lines of sweat rolling down the side of his face. Finally, he blurted out, "Fine. I'll tell you all I know."

Cedric released his hold and took a step back, his arms folded together. He nodded once, a silent command for Jasper to resume speaking.

"A couple of days ago, a strange man approached me asking if I was looking to earn a quick pay," Jasper began, adjusting the wrinkled collar of his shirt. "As you well know, I have little money to my name. I expressed my interest, and he asked me to find a way to sabotage your relationship with Anne."

"You're pathetic," Cedric spat out, too disgusted by his cousin's actions to mince words. "You betrayed my trust for only a few pounds."

"I have to admit my gambling has gotten out of hand," Jasper said, glancing down at the ground.

"It's too late to show contrition," Cedric retorted. "As a reward for your behavior, I promise to commit you to an institution."

With that statement, he left his brooding cousin in the garden and made his way toward the front of his house. His carriage sat waiting, and he wasted no time in boarding it.

He glanced out the window with unseeing eyes as the vehicle traveled along the streets of London. The roads were lit with lamps, and people were occupied with their respective lives. He was aware that every individual experienced turmoil and obstacles, but at the moment, it seemed like his own problems were foremost.

Who had paid Jasper to interfere in his relationship with Anne? One thing was certain, that person served to gain more from seeing them separated than being together. And if something wasn't done about it, Cedric would find himself or Anne being sabotaged over and over.

Cedric's carriage stopped at Greene's, a popular club for titled gentlemen. He rarely visited, but moments like this called for a social environment accompanied by a strong glass of whiskey.

He found a seat and signaled a server, dully expressing his order. Just as he finished doing that, his friends Lords Haynes and Cobridge approached his table.

"Why do you look so morose?" Haynes asked with a raised eyebrow.

"I have just had the most horrid day of my life," Cedric answered.

"This is my first time seeing you look so distraught," Cobridge said worriedly. "Is this about Lady Anne? Tell us what the matter is."

"My relationship with Anne is entirely ruined. I fear I may be unable to salvage it."

His friends went quiet for what seemed like a long moment before Haynes broke the silence, his voice firm. "Tell us everything that occurred without skipping a single step."

Cedric didn't need to be told twice. He began with the pieces of information Haynes already knew, such as the attempt on Anne's life, before explaining the development of his and Anne's relationship and the recent disastrous dinner.

"Your cousin is a halfwit, the dumbest of the lot," Cobridge surmised, shaking his head. "It's a shame Blackwood is away from London. Otherwise, we might have convinced him to include Jasper in his prized retinue of exotic animals."

"The man is completely dimwitted," Haynes agreed. "Before we consider what to do about him, you must explain yourself to Anne and win her heart back."

Cedric groaned, taking a hard gulp of his drink. "I feel as though it's already lost."

"Not if you haven't informed her of Jasper's deception. She's likely angry and confused at the moment. You must explain your cousin's involvement and his intent to sabotage the relationship," Cobridge advised.

"In the meantime, I shall conduct more investigations regarding the strange individual who bribed Jasper into doing his bidding," Haynes said, frowning. "I suspect this matter may be linked to the attempt at the dig."

A server brought more glasses of brandy and set them on the table. Cedric grabbed one and took a long gulp.

"You're correct. It's much too organized to be a coincidence."

Cobridge placed an encouraging hand on his shoulder. "Let Haynes handle that while you explain yourself to Anne. If you succeed in that, all of this will no doubt become a matter of the past."

Cedric nodded, feeling slightly better. "Very well. I'll visit Anne tomorrow."

"I didn't think you were such a motivational individual," Haynes remarked to Cobridge.

"I'm an artist. It comes with the trade," Cobridge responded, leaning back in his seat with a grin on his face.

"It has been especially beneficial in this situation," Cedric murmured.

Cobridge's grin grew wider. "I wish you luck tomorrow. You'll require lots of it."

Chapter Twenty

Cedric showed up at the Eversley townhouse as early as he could manage without it being inappropriate. The sky looked dull and gray, with no hint of the sun. In a way, it mirrored how he'd felt watching Anne rush away from him the previous day.

However, thanks to his friends' encouragement, he felt a better future could still be salvaged. His feelings for Anne were genuine, so strong that his heart raced uncontrollably at the thought of her. Even in the unlikely instance that he didn't feel that way, he was simply too wealthy to covet a few artifacts.

He understood how precious the artifacts were to Anne. There was no reason for him to conspire to get them illegally. He was simply too wealthy to need to do so; their sale would be a drop in a sea of his financial assets. Looking back at it now, Jasper's story was utterly silly and unimaginative.

Anne's reaction was less about his cousin's statement and more about his silence in the face of the accusations. Other than asking a few vague questions, he hadn't vehemently rejected the notion that he was secretly manipulating Anne for monetary benefits.

Cedric understood why she would be upset. He could only hope Haynes and Cobridge were correct in their advice. He did not consider himself a skilled orator, but he was determined to speak genuinely and express himself coherently.

He returned a passing valet's greetings as he approached the arched entrance and knocked. An image of his present endeavor ending in failure crossed his mind, sending chills through him. If Anne were to reject his efforts at forgiveness, he would be destroyed completely. Utterly.

The door opened, revealing a solemn-looking Barnaby. The butler cast him a disappointed glance before speaking. "Good day, sir. How may I help you?"

"Good day, Barnaby. I'm here to see Anne."

"I'm afraid she isn't present, sir," Barnaby responded.

"She's out?" Cedric asked, his eyebrows furrowed in puzzlement. "In that case, I would be willing to wait until she returns."

"She isn't emotionally ready to attend to visitors," Barnaby clarified, a regretful edge in his tone. "I'm sorry, Lord Stonehaven, but you must take your leave now."

The butler's words were self-explanatory. The Eversleys had given orders for him not to be admitted into the house. He couldn't exactly blame them for that, although he wasn't willing to take the decision lying down either.

Spurred by the momentary obstacle in his path, Cedric made his way to the side of the house, where he was certain Anne's bedroom was. If he couldn't get inside the house to speak to her, then he would initiate a conversation from his position outside.

There were no guarantees that she would entertain his actions, but it was still better to try.

"Anne, are you there?" He called, but there was no answer. She could easily be somewhere else, such as the drawing room or garden. Yet, a part of Cedric suspected she was present in the bedroom but unwilling to speak to him.

He cleared his throat, quelling the anxious sensation in his chest before continuing, "I understand that you do not wish to speak to me. I don't blame you for that. My cousin spoke a great falsehood, and I was too stunned to respond properly."

There remained an almost deafening silence, loaded and accusatory in its stillness. If Anne was listening to him, then the few lines he'd uttered had done nothing to assure her of his innocence.

"Jasper claims an individual paid him off to sabotage the relationship you and I share," Cedric divulged. "He waited until he was certain you were present before making those ridiculous statements. Anne, I know how greatly you value your employment at the dig. I know those artifacts mean a great deal to you, and I would never hurt you by stealing them from you."

He thought he heard a soft gasp from the window, but he couldn't be certain. "The bond you and I share is real. It has always been real. You're a driven woman with great intellect, and I have always admired your inner strength. I'd no sooner swim through a blazing sea than attempt to downplay or sabotage your efforts."

Cedric paused, weighing his next words as he prepared to utter them. They were his most true, innermost thoughts. Stating them would leave him vulnerable. He could only hope that his openness was well worth it.

"I love you, Anne," he continued passionately. "Every inch and piece of you. I cannot imagine what my life would be without you in it. You are the color that brightens my world. Things have begun to pale quickly without you in it. I promised you a lovely dinner with my family, but that was sullied, and I apologize from the bottom of my heart. Allow me to make up for it with more dinners to come."

As Cedric finished speaking, he held his breath for anything, be it a sheet of paper or the sound of a voice. At last, he heard a noise from Anne's bedroom, a resounding confirmation that she'd been listening to every word he said.

***

Anne sat at her desk, glancing down at the pen that had fallen seconds ago from her grasp. She had been busy journaling her thoughts when she heard Cedric's voice at her window. It had come as a surprise, given that she'd never expected him to approach her again. She could only assume he'd resorted to seeking her attention in such a manner due to being turned away at the door.

Her family, having learned about what occurred, must have given strict instructions to Barnaby not to let Cedric in. It was their own little way of showing their support of her.

In any case, she'd been startled when he began speaking below her window. The more she listened, the more her surprise grew. It came as unexpected news to learn that Jasper had been deceitful regarding Cedric's motives. Although she was taken aback by Jasper's actions, it was a relief to know Cedric was always an honest, faithful man.

When he got the part about being in love with her, Anne found herself tearing up, and her pen clattered to the floor. Hers was both an emotional and physical reaction to the beautiful, poetic statements being sent in her direction.

Cedric loved her. Not a vague, idealistic image of a beautiful woman born into an equally elite family. Not because being married to her would be considered a perfect match in the eyes of society. His feelings for her went far beyond any selfish tendencies or unkind endeavors. They were raw and honest, romantic and selfless.

And she? She loved him as much as the sun loved the earth, rising each morning to view its endless beauty. She used to consider intellectual pursuits more important than anything else, but now her feelings for Cedric loomed dominant.

Cedric's confession was the perfect balm to heal her broken heart. She was more than relieved to learn that the previous night's encounter was all a mistake on Cedric's part. He had been wrong to trust his cousin blindly and would likely be more cautious henceforth.

"Anne?" She heard him call softly again, his voice full of warmth and concern. For as long as she lived, she hoped to hear him utter her name over and over.

Anne leapt to her feet and hurried down the winding staircase. Tessa was standing in the main hallway, a bright smile on her face.

"Did you hear him?" She whispered, her smile growing wider.

Anne nodded, her heart too filled with happiness to manage a response. She wished there was a way to document his confession word for word, preserving it in history long after they were both gone.

"Those were the most beautiful sentiments I have ever heard anyone utter," Tessa confessed, wiping a lone tear from her cheek. "Go to him, Anne."

Anne didn't need to be told twice. She managed a brief nod before exiting the house and hurrying in Cedric's direction. He spun around as she approached, his eyes widening with pleasure.

"Anne, I'm sorry for—"

"You don't need to apologize. Not anymore," Anne cut in, drawing closer until they were separated by only a few yards. "None of what occurred was entirely your fault."

He shook his head and ran a hand through his hair. " I should have been more careful, more observant regarding my cousin's antics. He should never have had a chance to hurt you so."

"He'll never get that opportunity again," Anne replied. "I bear no grudges, and I'm glad you're here. How did you know I was present in my bedroom? I could be anywhere else."

"I wasn't certain you were listening, actually," Cedric revealed. "I just wanted to give it a try regardless."

Her cheeks burned red, and she palmed her face shyly. "That was incredibly brave of you."

He took a step closer, reaching for her hand and holding it tightly. "It was more a necessity than anything else. I couldn't bear to be away from you any longer and was willing to take any chance."

Anne had no reason to doubt his words, especially not when his lovely gray eyes were alight with honesty.

"You have expressed your feelings, and now it's time for me to do the same."

"I assure you, it's alright. There are no expectations for you to reciprocate—"

"I want to," she cut in, smiling warmly at him. "I have wanted to do this for quite a while."

"When did you realize you felt this way?"

Anne considered the question as several memories from the past lingered in her mind.

"I cannot say for certain. I suppose it's a combination of many things, such as your consideration for others, attentiveness, and brilliant sense of humor. I had no idea I was slowly growing enamored with you until it bloomed into something full-fledged."

"I hope this interest continues to grow," Cedric said with a pleased grin. "Nothing makes me happier than being the focus of your attention."

"It isn't merely interest," Anne corrected. "It's more than that. I love you, Cedric, with all my heart."

It was a daring confession, but the significant transformation of his handsome face made it all worthwhile. Cedric looked the happiest she'd ever seen him, a broad smile inching along his face.

"I love you, Anne, and I shall continue to love you the rest of my days," he responded, his voice heavy with emotion. "Will you marry me? Now that I have you, it feels excruciatingly unfair to be separated for even a second longer."

Anne blinked rapidly to keep the threatening swarm of tears at bay, but one rolled down her cheek nonetheless. "The answer is yes. I will marry you today and always."

"I have never loved anyone else. I will never love anyone else," Cedric vowed, covering the distance and gently tucking a strand of hair behind her ears.

In one fluid movement, he sealed his promise with a dizzying, long kiss. It was absolutely perfect, full of unspoken dreams of a joyous future. She was stunned, grateful, and happy all at once, amazed by a kiss that was miles better than she'd ever imagined.

"That was ... mind-blowing," Anne said after they drew apart and she finally caught her breath.

"There will be better ones as time passes," Cedric assured her with a wink.

"My family, especially my aunt, will be overjoyed to learn of our engagement."

"The same can be said of my mother. She adores you, so this will be thrilling news for her."

Anne giggled. "With any luck, Bernice and Lady Lavinia will work together to oversee the wedding plans."

"Without a doubt, they'll be at each other's throats," Cedric concluded in an amused tone. "It will be quite an interesting wedding indeed."

They strolled toward the garden whilst holding hands, the wind carrying the sounds of their voices as they planned the details of their future together.

Chapter Twenty-One

Anne sat at her table, inattentively flipping through the pages of a book. She couldn't keep from smiling, her mind filled with thoughts of the previous day. Her entire interaction with Cedric seemed almost like it had come from the pages of a romance book, except hers was real and exhilarating.

He wanted her. Not as a friend or an individual enlisted to keep his mother from nagging about marriage. He had asked to marry her, expressing his feelings in long, precise statements that kept her heart racing hours after they'd been uttered.

All her life, she'd prioritized the love of her family and the company of her books. It had been difficult to conceive that anyone else, be it a husband or fiancé, would ever fill a position of similar importance in her life. Against all odds, Cedric had woven his way into her soul, where he would remain permanently.

She was looking forward to a happy future spent teaching him significant facts about history and paying visits to his stud farm. It was expected that her family would be pleased by news of the engagement, but their reaction was so very positive that it shocked Anne as well.

Bernice chattered nonstop about her plans for the wedding, vowing it would be the talk of all London. Her uncle was relieved she had acquired a gentleman who, in his words, was "sensible and charming enough to endear himself to the entire world if he wished." It was nice to overhear him offering his planning skills to Bernice should she need any assistance.

Meanwhile, Tessa narrated the previous evening's events to anyone who cared to listen, her eyes growing shinier as she emphasized certain sentences in Cedric's passionate speech. And Alix, witty, deadpan Alix, had taken to talking and smiling more.

I cannot pause to imagine what my life would be without you in it.

Those words from Cedric would always remain in her mind, right next to his request for her to marry him. To someone else, they might seem like simple statements, but she recognized and understood the emotional weight that lay within them.

Marriage was considered the most important part of a woman's life in conventional society. As far as rules went, Anne had secured a perfect prospect for herself. However, for her, it went beyond wealth and titles. It mattered more that Cedric was as gentle as he was loving.

The arrival of a maid brought her out of her thoughts. "I have come to deliver a message from your uncle, my lady."

"Feel free to share."

"He has requested that you meet him at a shoe store for a quick fitting. A coachman awaits you downstairs and will take you there. Shall I help you prepare for your outing?"

"That won't be necessary. Thank you," Anne responded. Glad she was already dressed in functional clothes, she secured a bonnet over her head and stepped out of the room. It was unusual for her uncle to send for her without warning, but it wasn't entirely out of place.

Perhaps, in his excitement, he wished to show her around the store. With that thought in mind, Anne made her way down the stairs and past the door. A carriage sat waiting, with a different design than she was used to seeing.

Her uncle had spoken earlier about purchasing new carriages, therefore the vehicle didn't seem out of place. With the help of a valet with his hat tipped low over his head, she climbed into the coach. As she sat on the plush seat, the valet climbed in before securing the carriage doors shut.

"You might want to think twice before screaming for help," he said in a threatening tone, a silver-tipped pistol aimed at her. "I have got a weapon, and I'm not averse to using it."

The man's voice was strangely familiar, but Anne's mind was racing too fast to consider the topic further. Instead, she nodded to show she understood.

"Turn around and place your hands behind you," the man ordered roughly. "Otherwise, I'll hurt you."

Anne shivered involuntarily. Something in the man's voice told her he meant every word and would not hesitate to harm her if the situation called for it. She was terrified of him, her thoughts conjuring a thousand ways he could hurt her.

If she desired to get out of this alive, she was left with no choice but to cooperate. It would only be a strategy, lulling him into believing she was dull and harmless until a good opportunity for escape arose.

"There's no need for that. I'll do as you ask," she replied, careful to keep the fear out of her voice.

Anne turned to face the wall, and as she waited for the man's next orders, a sharp pain registered in the side of her neck before darkness consumed her.

***

The low hum of conversing voices buzzed around Cedric as he sat alone at a table at Greene's. He could hardly pay attention to the environment, too overcome by a unique and pleasurable thrum of joy. Anne had not only accepted his apology, she'd also given her assent to marriage. Once they had finalized plans with their families, a grand wedding would follow, their gateway to a life lived happily together.

As more such happy thoughts swam in his mind, he was barely aware of a server pausing at his table.

"What would you like to have, sir?" the man asked dully.

Cedric shook his head, a bright smile playing on his lips. "There will be no alcoholic drinks for me today, I'm afraid. Life is much too amazing to be dulled by tart intoxicants."

"In that case, might you be interested in some tea or coffee?"

The idea seemed more appealing, so Cedric nodded. "Tea would be nice. Earl Grey, preferably."

While he awaited his tea, he thought about how brilliantly his life was turning out. He'd never felt more at peace despite once vowing that he had no intention of marrying young. All he wanted now was to have Anne by his side, hear the sound of her laughter, and experience the warmth of her presence.

A shadow above him interrupted his musing. He glanced up to find Cobridge standing only a few feet away, peering at him curiously. "Why were you staring off into the distance with a smile on your face?"

"I did that?"

"Indeed," Cobridge replied, taking a seat. "I only approached because you were familiar to me, and we've been friends for several years. Anyone else would have assumed you were thoroughly demented."

Another smile traveled along Cedric's face. "We certainly can't have that, not when I have a wedding to prepare for."

"Correct. We certainly cannot—" Cobridge's jaw dropped midway through the sentence. "Your wedding or another's?"

"Mine," he replied as the server set his tea on the table. "I asked Anne to marry me, and she said yes."

"Brilliant!" Cobridge exclaimed, giving him a congratulatory pat on the shoulder. "I never thought you'd be the first of us to be married, but I can see how happy this makes you."

"My joy has no boundaries," Cedric admitted. "It's like being on a luxurious voyage with ample resources, except this time, the good parts are gathered into one individual."

"Lady Anne sounds like an amazing human indeed. However, seeing you has further validated my hunch that love is potentially dangerous," Cobridge stated, waving a server over.

Cedric took a sip of his tea. "Why is that the case?"

"Only a while ago, you looked like the world was ending, and now—brandy, please," he paused to mutter his drink preference to the server before resuming. "You're the perfect image of a satisfactory life."

"Mark my words, love is only terrible when things aren't in order. Otherwise, it's the most wonderful experience a person can have," Cedric told his friend.

"Hm," Cobridge said as if giving the matter some thought. "Anyway, you have Haynes and me to thank for urging you to see her after you were convinced the relationship was ruined."

"That is correct," Cedric replied. "As a show of my appreciation, I vow to interfere positively in your future relationships if they happen to go sour."

Cobridge reached for his drink the second it arrived. "I doubt you'll have cause to do so anytime soon. My heart will remain untouched for the foreseeable future."

"I suppose we'll see," Cedric said, unconvinced.

"Why have you come here anyway? Shouldn't you be celebrating the engagement elsewhere?"

"I had every intention of doing so when I received a message from Haynes requesting that we meet at Greene's."

"That's rather unusual. He's not one to dally and be late to arranged meets," Cobridge remarked.

Cedric nodded. "You're right. He isn't in the habit of delaying others, which is why I'm waiting so patiently."

"In the meantime, perhaps we can discuss something else. Have you heard the latest news regarding the Parliament?"

"No. I left the house early this morning with no time to read the paper."

"It appears a new law is being discussed regarding the length of corsets. Ridiculous topic, don't you think? If I had my way, I would—"

"Good evening," a gruff, authoritative voice belonging to Haynes interrupted.

"You have arrived at a good time," Cedric said. "Cobridge was just about to launch into another tirade about the parliamentary members."

"A good number are men of power with little substance," Haynes said in agreement, taking a seat. "However, the subject of our discussion tonight is more urgent and personal."

Cedric tensed at his friend's grave tone. "What did you discover?"

"My investigation of Anne's attacker revealed his identity as a middle-class gentleman operating out of an office on King Street. He isn't very well-liked and as of yet, very little has been discovered regarding his motive."

"Will you arrest him right away?" Cobridge asked.

Haynes shook his head. "Not yet. I have tasked some men with tracking his movements. I'm convinced he'll act in an incriminating manner soon."

Before Cedric could say anything else, he noticed a young woman approaching their table. She pulled back her hood, revealing a familiar, solemn face belonging to Polly, Anne's maid.

Cedric rose to his feet, his voice urgent. "Did something happen?"

"Yes, my lord," Polly replied, her face wet with tears. "Lady Anne has been abducted."

Cedric suddenly felt lightheaded but steeled himself to remain standing. This was not a silly prank or joke. It was a severe situation, and Anne's life depended on how rationally he behaved.

"Tell me how," Haynes urged. "And be careful not to leave a single detail out."

The distressed maid tearfully narrated how Anne had been lured out by a false letter from her uncle before being driven away in an unfamiliar carriage. She left the club as quietly as she'd arrived after being convinced by Haynes that everything would be alright.

"The same goes for you, too," Haynes said to Cedric as they departed the building.

"I'm not heading home until this matter has been resolved," Cedric said firmly.

Haynes shook his head. "I'm not asking you to. I only need you to remain calm and logical. If we're going to save Anne, we'll need all our senses."

"Cedric is undoubtedly hurting at the moment, but I believe he's a hundred percent ready to find his fiancée's abductor," Cobridge spoke up.

"And you? Will you join us on this potentially dangerous mission?"

Cobridge nodded. "Of course. What sort of person would I be if I went to bed while my friends were risking their lives?"

"Very well," Haynes replied. His black coach stopped on the street, and they all climbed in. "Given all I have discovered, it isn't too farfetched to assume the same man who tried to kill Anne has now abducted her. We'll need to track them quickly before irrevocable harm is done."

Chapter Twenty-Two

Anne awakened with a groan, her head throbbing from pain. Her limbs ached as she rose from the bare floor into a sitting position. The last thing she remembered was climbing into the carriage before a surge of darkness overwhelmed her. A strange man posing as a valet had tricked her into believing her uncle had sent for her. Why had he done so? The answer was a complete mystery. As far as she knew, there was little reason for anyone to act so harshly toward her.

She opened her eyes and surveyed her environment, her heart beating fearfully in her chest. She was in a moderately sized room with a closed door and one window, through which the full moon shone as the only source of light. There was no furniture other than a bookshelf placed at the far end of the room.

Whoever abducted her had planned carefully. The surrounding deafening silence told her she was in an isolated spot and no one would find her, no matter how much she screamed. It was a thoroughly haunting realization, so she took slow breaths to retain her composure.

The door opened without warning, and a lone figure walked in. Through the slight blur of her vision, she made out his lanky body and distorted grin. The man standing in front of her was none other than Lawry, the ill-dressed man she had encountered at the museum. He was still wearing the valet clothing he had kidnapped her in; his hat tilted higher to reveal more of his face.

Now, he was staring down at her with a triumphant look, his thin lips pulling aside to reveal awfully maintained rows of teeth.

"It appears you're finally awake," he began, folding his arms. "I considered letting you remain conscious through the journey, but you kept speaking nonstop. Luckily, I didn't have to hit you. You were knocked asleep by an effective concoction I purchased."

"Why did you abduct me?" Anne asked. As far as she knew, there had been no further interactions since the museum. She'd not acted in a manner to provoke his aggressive actions.

"Aren't you supposed to be intelligent? The answer to your question is quite obvious."

Anne's eyebrows furrowed in confusion. "Frankly, I cannot think of any reason. We only met once, and I've had no other interactions with you."

"You wealthy dimwits are only able to consider yourselves and no other," Lawry commented, his face twisting with disgust.

"I'm trying to understand, so please tell me what your objections are."

By urging him to reply to her question, Anne hoped to get a thorough explanation for his behavior. She could only hope that doing so would not aggravate him and place her further in danger.

"Very well," Lawry replied, a crazed glint in his eye. "I suppose it doesn't matter whether I explain it or not. I have no intention of letting you live after this, so I might as well satisfy your curiosity."

"I'm all ears," she managed to say, although her heart raced even faster upon hearing his statement.

"Spoilt heiress that you are, you cannot know how difficult it is for a man with no titles and little wealth to climb the social ladder," Lawry said in an accusatory tone.

Anne hesitated before replying, "I have a fair idea based on the books I read and the experience I have gained from conversations."

"That pales in comparison to living that life firsthand," her abductor retorted. "I overcame a great number of odds to become a revered secretary at the Society of Antiquaries of London. Some noblemen, believing I was a mere commoner with little worth, antagonized me, but I fought them off to reach my position today."

She held her breath as she listened, curious but also anxious about what he would say next. It was not inconceivable that a man would rise in status, although it was difficult in present English society. As much as she understood the struggle Lawry must have gone through, she was confused as to what it had to do with her.

"My position is not an easy one. We secretaries are tasked with physical labor while the so-called learned gentlemen turn up their noses and pore over their books," Lawry continued, his voice filled with disgust. "We are the ones who go out to the fields and deliver the antiques to the museums. We're the ones people reach out to when they have concerns or objections. It's a stressful, thankless job."

"I understand your life is incredibly difficult, but your narration baffles me. Did you abduct me to gain a ransom?" Anne inquired.

"A ridiculous notion," Lawry responded with a dismissive wave of his hand. "I would not have resorted to abducting you if the poisoning attempt had worked."

"Why then did you try to poison me?"

"You ruined my entire plans, a spoiled heiress playing at being a historian," Lawry spat. "All you had to do was do a shoddy job of examining the antiques, and all would have turned out well."

Was he blaming her for being a capable worker? Anne tried to keep from replying, but the urge was simply too strong to resist. "The Society hired me to determine whether the antiques were real or fake. I carried out my duties efficiently."

Lawry's cruel eyes dug uncomfortably into her. "And look where that got you. Stuck in a room with me, vulnerable and isolated from family."

"I did as I was asked," Anne said firmly. "I made no attempts to harm anyone."

"By spreading the news that the artifacts are real, you ruined my chance to sell them and grow wealthy," Lawry finished. "Now they'll be taken to a museum to gather dust. However, you will be punished for all I have lost."

With that final statement tossed over his shoulder, he strolled out of the room. Alone in the haunting silence left over, she glanced up at the ceiling thoughtfully. Although she was terrified, she began devising a plan to escape.

***

Cedric said an internal prayer as the carriage sped along dirt-strewn paths. They were in an unwelcoming part of London, filled with abandoned buildings and sparse dwellings. Thankfully, they did not have to waste time checking each house. One of Haynes' men had provided a tip regarding where Anne was being kept.

He could only hope they'd get to her in time. There was no telling what horrors the man who abducted her had planned. He needed to rescue her before irrevocable damage occurred, turning every aspect of Anne's life into a terrible play.

"We're here," Haynes announced as the carriage slowed to a stop. "Are you two ready?"

"What does 'ready' mean?" Cobridge questioned. "We could use a plan of action. Do we simply barge into the building? Or wait for more men to arrive?"

"That won't do," Cedric responded with a shake of his head. "I cannot wait outside a second longer, not when Anne's safety isn't guaranteed."

"We won't wait," Haynes reassured him, retrieving a bag beneath the carriage seats. He pulled out three pistols, ensuring each man had one. "They're loaded and efficient for quickdraws. I encourage you both to use them wisely. We do not want unwanted injuries or deaths."

"Luckily, I'm a decent shot," Cobridge said, eyeing the pistol. "Might I ask why you, a classed gentleman with no criminal history, have a bag of pistols hidden in your vehicle?"

"No, you can't. We have a hostage to rescue," Haynes replied.

Cobridge's face turned serious. "Very well. I shall postpone the question for later."

Cedric was too consumed by his concern for Anne to contribute to the conversation. He pushed the carriage door open and descended onto the muddy street. A lone building with a metal door towered above, exuding a threatening energy.

He walked over to the door and turned the knob, disappointment overcoming him when he realized it was locked.

"A building this large is bound to have another entrance," Haynes muttered. "Let's try the back."

Cobridge dug into his pockets for an item before stepping forward. "There's no need for that. I am rather skilled at picking locks."

Cedric watched with a mix of apprehension and momentary relief as his friend worked the lock. A minute later, there was a clicking sound, and the door slowly inched open.

The men entered the house, careful not to make any loud sounds. Lit lamps strategically placed along the walls and moonlight pouring in through the windows helped them see.

"There's no telling where Anne is being kept," Cobridge whispered. "There are over a dozen rooms in this building."

The unmistakable sound of footsteps could be heard above, and it sounded like they were heading their way. That was the confirmation Cedric needed.

"I have a hunch the direction of those footsteps is where Anne is," Cedric murmured. "I need you two to distract or apprehend him while I find Anne."

"Will you be able to handle that alone?" Haynes asked.

"I won't stop looking until I find her. That's the only trait I need," Cedric replied.

While Haynes and Cobridge busied themselves with distracting or apprehending the man, whichever came first, Cedric rushed in the opposite direction. He went up the stairs, his pistol firmly in his hands, while he checked each room quickly and carefully.

With each room he passed, his concern for Anne grew stronger. He opened the final room in the upper corridor, wishing desperately that it would contain the woman he loved.

"Cedric?" A familiar voice belonging to none other than Anne said. She was sitting in a corner of the room, holding a metal item.

Her dress was dust-stained, and blonde hair spilled messily around her shoulders. Despite that, to him, she was the most beautiful woman in the world.

"I'm so relieved to find you," Cedric said, walking over and drawing her into a hug.

"I am so happy you're here," Anne replied with teary, joy-filled eyes. She glanced briefly at the metal object in her hand. "I was halfway through twisting my hairpin into a tool for picking the lock when you arrived. No matter how nice that plan sounded, it pales in comparison to your presence."

She glanced up at him with so much love in her eyes; he wished he could preserve that look forever.

Haynes and Cobridge appeared in the doorway, both looking solemn but accomplished.

"During our altercation with the abductor, we managed to take his weapon and subdue him," Haynes announced. "He won't be bothering anyone anymore. You two should depart this building before it inevitably becomes an investigation scene in a couple of hours. Cobridge and I will await the constable's arrival."

"I'm relieved he'll be arrested," Anne murmured, taking Cedric's hand. "I'd like to leave as soon as possible."

Cedric didn't need to be asked twice. He led her out of the house and helped her into the carriage while thinking of how to express the thoughts in his head. Anne's abduction had only confirmed further what he already knew: that he was madly in love with her and wanted to marry her without delay.

"I wish we could be married right away," Anne said as if reading his thoughts. "While I was abducted, beyond my fear of being harmed, I was also terrified that I'd never see you again."

"I felt the same way," Cedric replied, smiling brightly as he reached for her hands. "However, our mothers will have extensive fits if we elope without their knowledge. I love you, Anne."

"Does that mean we'll be married soon?"

He nodded. "I shall arrange for our families to meet and become familiar with one another before planning the wedding the following week."

She returned his smile with a bigger, brighter one. "I'll be sure to appear in my best dress."

Cedric chuckled, placing a chaste kiss on her cheek. "Undoubtedly, you'll be the most stunning bride anyone ever witnessed."

As the carriage raced ahead, they became lost in each other's caring gazes, having found a love so great it defied reason.

Epilogue

The sun shone brightly, casting the sky in shades of gold and blue. Birds perched in trees chirped songs of merriment. A buzz of anticipation rose in the air as people garbed in impressive finery gathered at a grand church building.

It was the best day of Anne's life. Things had changed immensely since the day she found herself wondering if Cedric shared the same romantic feelings as she did. He had not only proven his love for her, he was now sealing it in full view of everyone.

Nothing could wipe the bright, happy smile from Anne's face as she walked down the aisle. Her aunt and Lady Lavinia had certainly outdone themselves. After a few skirmishes, the two women eventually agreed on a breathtaking gown that drew all eyes to it.

Woven from an elaborate stretch of smooth cream-colored lace and styled in a high collar cut, it sat perfectly atop her skin. Her hair held up with pins, the rest falling along the side of her face in soft curls.

Anne's heart sped up joyfully as she met Cedric's eyes. He looked dashing and handsome in his tailored suit, a wide grin planted permanently on his face. He was hers. Undeniably hers. As they stood together at the altar, he glanced at her with evident admiration and love.

There was no doubt in her mind that she was making the right decision. No one else had shown the same level of devotion to her or bared their heart out the way he did. Anne was aware that she was incredibly fortunate. Even in unpleasant times, Cedric would always put her first. He had expressed that time and time again before backing it up with actions.

If he hadn't rescued her when he did, Anne would no doubt remain missing or worse. There was no more fitting conclusion to their recent stress-filled experiences than a glorious wedding. Both their families were in attendance, garbed in their best outfits and wholly in support. Her uncle dabbed surreptitiously at his eyes with a handkerchief while her aunt looked on with pronounced triumph.

The priest smiled warmly, stepping forward as he began the ceremony.

"Anne, do you take Cedric, Earl of Stonehaven, to be your lawfully wedded husband?"

Happy tears swelled in the corner of Anne's eyes. She knew her answer already, and it flowed out of her mouth with ease. "I do."

"Cedric, Earl of Stonehaven, do you take Anne to be your lawfully wedded wife?" The priest inquired.

"I do," Cedric replied without missing a beat, his tone firm and confident.

The priest nodded satisfactorily, another smile crossing his face. "You have my blessing. Now join hands and repeat after me. I take thee to be my wedded wife or husband. To have and to hold from this day forward. For better or for worse, for richer, for poorer, in sickness and in health, to love and cherish, till death do us part."

Cedric winked at her as he set his hands forward, urging her to place hers atop his. She did so without hesitation, delighted by the comforting warmth of his skin.

"I, Anne, take thee to my wedded husband," Anne began, flushing in pleasure as Cedric joined her with his own slightly altered statement, their voices intertwined in a pleasant lilt. "To have and to hold, from this day forward. For better or for worse, for richer, for poorer, in sickness and in health, to love and cherish, till death do us part."

"I pronounce you husband and wife. You may now kiss the bride," the priest declared.

Mesmerized by Cedric's soft, affectionate look, Anne allowed herself to be pulled into his strong arms as his lips captured hers in a stupefying kiss. The congregation erupted in loud applause and encouraging cheers.

Anne knew there and then that she'd found the best item for premium living: a love so precious it exceeded all the gold in the world—and she was determined to preserve it forever.

THE END

Thank you for reading "Anne, Love Unearthed."

If you loved this book, you will love the first book in my Somersley Series Entitled "Governess Penelope and a Duke!"

It's a feel-good story about an unexpected second chance with a first love.

Click here and get your FREE copy of "Governess Penelope and a Duke": https://dl.bookfunnel.com/a5l15u9hpa

In 1811 London, Penelope, a governess disowned by her father, discovers love while preparing her friend's niece for society.

This full-length second-chance romance offers a happily-ever-after ending,

Click here and get your FREE copy of Governess Penelope and a Duke now! https://dl.bookfunnel.com/a5l15u9hpa

PLEASE LEAVE A REVIEW FOR "Anne, Love Unearthed".

https://www.amazon.com/review/create-review?&asin=B0DJ9TGFDK

Printed in Dunstable, United Kingdom